THE TRIUMPH
OF CHRISTIANITY

THE TRIUMPH
OF CHRISTIANITY

Tales of Good and Evil

Joseph P. Policape

To order additional copies of this book, contact:
Xlibris
844-714-8691
www.Xlibris.com
Orders@Xlibris.com
829408

CONTENTS

INTRODUCTION

"BAINET!" WAS THE strong whisper under his breath, and this took him on a trip to the wide-open universe of his past. Every time he looked back, he couldn't help but fall on his knees and praise God's son, Jesus Christ, for what he had done for him and his family.

Mario was nearing his forty-seventh birthday. He was sitting in his favorite rocking chair, thinking about his one great passion, the Christian Church, and how Christianity had saved him from the tentacles of Satan and his supporters.

In those days, the whole town seemed to have become the servant of the demonic spirit of vodou. Christianity, or rather, Roman Catholicism, had made its peace with this religion of possession although it was not done purposefully but because, during the '60s, Papa Doc expelled all non-Haitian priests out of the Catholic Church. And later on, when he asked to be reinstated in the church, he demanded that he would only hire Haitian priests. Haitian priests took control of the Catholic Church, and with that, he also instilled vodou culture and it is the practice within it to this day.

But a small band of Protestants, Pentecostal in spirit and early Christians in faith, started a war against vodou, and Mario's mother joined that righteous band of Jesus lovers. And that changed his life forever.

Slowly at first, but with increasing authority and religious force, they saved many citizens of Bainet from the spiritual shackles of vodou and the seemingly limitless powers of Satan.

Today was a bit harder for Mario because of these flooding memories. They were like a clear stream cascading through his mind and heart. Once he got up from his bed, all in good health, and washed himself and waited not long for his niece to fix his breakfast, he found himself walking to his porch with the dreams of his past heavy upon his mind and heart.

He seemed to be two persons today, a distant neighbor and a very close neighbor to himself who he heard his voice, and then somebody else's voice was heard above his head. To know that it was not him speaking though he knew that both voices were his voices, he felt that God was the voice he couldn't figure out earlier. And these voices pointed to his responsibility to tell all the stories that were stored up in his mind and heart, how Pentecostalism won the victory against the brutal and manipulative deception of vodou worship and magic.

The second voice wanted to remind him of how long it had been, and that now was the time to get the stories out there in the world and to the people of Bainet. His head was a whole library of stories, and before his dearest mother passed, she made him promise that he would sit down and tell these stories, or she would isolate him within the wounds and happiness of time to write the church's stories for posterity.

The day was so beautifully bright and warm for Mario, almost like the day when his mother went off to eternity. Hers was such an easy and peaceful death. Looking up at the morning sun, he knew this was going to be a very different day and that his mother was going to dominate in his thoughts.

"Tell our stories, my child," she told him, gazing in his soul and yet already at the right hand of God.

Mario remembered how he had leaned over and touched her forehead with his lips and squeezed her left hand as a promise to give each account of how Christ and his band of warriors took on all of vodou's protectors, including the corrupt and murderous government.

Nobody came on that porch, and his niece, after giving him a midmorning breakfast, had left for the market. Mario continued to sit long enough to see nature bring some slight rain followed by a lovely mist to the day. He was pleased that the clear day was erased from the sky and was replaced with this dark mist, so the world couldn't see his tears of joy for the life of his mother. He could hear her now, saying "God has blessed us to find the way and to show others the way too, my child."

Next Thursday would mark the third year since she had been called away to heaven. Only three years before, Mario was left with a stubborn, but infinitely fascinating man who was his father.

The father broke his mother's heart because, as her husband and as his father, he refused both pleas and rejected Christianity; he would not yield to their wish to believe in Jesus and Christianity. Ogou Feray, Danbala-Wedo, and Legba were his gods, and they would remain his gods even as she pleaded for him to convert on her deathbed. Vodou is what he worshipped, and it seemed that no amount of prayer or preaching or teaching of the holy word would change that.

Yes, he was a mystery, but not to God, and Mario strongly felt that he was left here on earth to bring the old man into the Christian fold. And when that was accomplished, his father would join his mother, and only then could he leave Bainet and minister somewhere else.

"It's not natural to sit for so long," he said to himself.

He got up with his plate and glass and walked back into his house, passed through the living and dining rooms to gain the kitchen, and placed his plate and glass into the sink, rinsing them and leaving them there. He needed a walk by the waters because he had convinced himself on that porch that he was going to do exactly what his mother had made him promise to do three years ago. He was going to make sure that the stories of the Christian Pentecostals like his mother and others would get out into the world. His stories and others would show the world how his mother's Christian Pentecostals had won a victory over Satan and vodou, miracles over magical illusions, human love over human misery, life over death.

The stories were going to be told in homage to the old saints and for the healing sake of the young generations in Bainet, those who were still dabbling in vodou for answers because they are still victims of fear and revenge.

So Mario would gather up these stories on the curse of Satan and the victory of Jesus Christ in Bainet. He had grown up in these two worlds with a father who was involved in vodou and a mother who had led him to Jesus Christ and Pentecostalism, the genuine and powerful

Christianity that took on and won the fight against Satan and his bloody and greedy helpers in Bainet.

All of Bainet knew he was a great storyteller and, just as important, a great listener. Here then you will find fourteen short tales. Some of these tales are told by Mario and some told by other Christian witnesses and some told by worshipers of vodou who turned to Jesus's truth after being led to salvation by the Christian Pentecostals. In each one of these wonderful tales, we find vodou to be a very powerful religion that only Jesus can undo and conquer. Everyone who reads these heartfelt tales will be affected by them one way or another.

THOSE VODOU GODS

EVERY HAITIAN CARRIES a bag filled with secrets of vodou gods they could not reveal. Danbala-Wedo is the benevolent *loa* (spirits) that filled us and enable us to say how we feel. Ayida-Wedo promises miracles to his horses. How did I get to be associated with such mysteries that I have heard? I regretted watching the sacrifice of black goats, cows, and pigs. The vèvè and magic diagram had been drawn before my eyes.

I had seen my mother filled with Loa Cousin and my aunt with AgweTawoyo, the spirit of the sea. How did I get to go to places filled with magic and demonic powers? Oh, I was young; Ogou Badagri wanted me to hold his spiced rhum. As I ran, he laughed; I saw blood in her mouth. I sat under the temple of Ougan to watch Erzilie Freda and Danto dance, and Marassa ate their meal and played with their toys. How dare I go that deep into the darkness? I heard of Kalfu, the hungry vodou god who controls the evil forces, laugh.

The mystic culture brought tears to my eyes, but with Jesus, I rise from such a disgrace. I now understand how blind I was before I found the essence of true grace. My ancestors were so blinded. They worshipped the stars and praised the sun. And now, the gods of my parents are Ghede, Simbi Dlo, and Legba. What a disgrace and curse to their children as worshipers of nature.

The gods suck the blood of my brothers, for Daddy had not paid them with a black goat? And my father still serves Azaca, the vodou god that walks barefoot wearing a black raincoat.

Thank you, heaven, for saving my soul from such a culture filled with ferocity. I was too young to have seen the mysterious powers of vodou, which, to my brain, was such a fatality. Those gods that some of us chose to serve are our curse, and they took away our peace.

Does Haiti look like Africa? Their gods make them war with each other and keep them in ceaseless conflict. Those mystery vodou gods caused many to live in fear, anger, and anxiety.

Ah, those whom Baron Samedi possessed and mounted became killers and apathetic. Why did anyone serve those devil gods who caused them to live in poverty and homelessness? Those vodou gods make Haitians, among all the Caribbean nations, live in hopelessness.

TALE 1

THE MASSACRE
AT BAMBOO

I T WAS IN April 1968, on a Thursday dawn, and the day had just exchanged position with the night. I saw the moon take her nightgown off, and I saw her going back to her chamber. Then I saw Ms. Day dressed in her pink robe as Mr. Sun came to meet her on his golden suit as he sang, "Hail to thee, Ms. Day!" Then I heard the rooster sing the four o'clock song when I heard a horse arriving on our premises, then a rich man by the name of Officer Belony knocked at our door.

It was just after the *vodouisant*, vodou priest Monier, finished feeding the dead and breaking the jugs in the month of April. And because Loa Cousin showed up at the ceremony and he was eaten before Brave Gede, Brave Gede promised a bloodbath in the area.

My father, known as Mr. Nicolas, got up in his blue pajamas, quickly put his dark night robe on, and asked, "Who is this?"

The children overheard the person answering, "This is Officer Belony." Then the glare of his flashlight blinded Daddy's eyes when he opened the door for the officer.

Officer Belony pushed the door wide open, and as he entered the house, so did the cold air. Belony pointed the gun at my daddy, and momentarily, my daddy's heart broke into little pieces.

Father found his voice and yelled, "What's up, man?"

"I'm just kidding," Officer Belony answered him. "I'm here to let you know, this morning, we are going to have a massacre at Bamboo."

Officer Belony stood proudly, and on his face was the disgust that he had for the future victims. "Well," the officer said, "we have had enough from the thieves in this commune. They steal everything we have. They think that we are rich, and we do not eat. I came here to see if you are hiding some of them."

Then Officer Belony laughed. "No, I know you would never hide any thieves in your house. We've got to kill them though, or they are going to destroy us by stealing our entire livelihood. I have a list of all the thieves in the area. I met with the other officers and every man of value in the area. You know them. You, me, and Lubin, we are the rich men in Zorangé. We are also the men of values. Even God knows that, but the thieves and the poor in this area feel they can disrespect us. Since they have no reverence for us, we are going to make them respect us once and for all. We are going to wipe them out forever in this commune. We shall slaughter them one by one. We shall create a bloodbath today. Lucifer shall descend to salute us after this bloodbath."

"Show me your list. Who do you have on it, may I ask?" Daddy inquired of Officer Belony.

"If you go down by the river right now, you will see them. We already arrested about 95 percent of them, and they're ready to be massacred. We should be ready to proceed with the slaughter around five o'clock this morning. Make sure you are there on time, Mr. Nicolas. I will make the first toss with you," Officer Belony said.

"Can you name a few of them that you already have on your list?" asked my father.

Officer Belony said, "Look!" He handed a list to Daddy. "I have Neresto, Jason, Lemonier, Wilson, Benjamin, Raymond, Lené, Joel who are some of the gang leaders," said Officer Belony.

Daddy took his three sons, including me, a twelve-year-old boy at the time, and walked us down the river to watch the massacre. We were afraid. Something was not right.

"Daddy, why did you wake us? And where are we going?"

"Sons, do not be afraid," Daddy assured us. "You are with me. There is going to be a massacre at Bamboo. The officers are going to be despicable, but do not be afraid of them. They are going to be furious while they beat the thieves, but you are men. You need to know about this stuff. You need to learn how the police react when they are enraged."

Along the path to the river, I pulled on my dad's pajamas. "Daddy, I see blood. I see a trail of blood from Risqué to the river of Zorangé. I see blood coming down the river. Is this the blood of Nereste, Jason, Lemonier, and Wilson?"

He saw how very upset I looked, and he said, "Son, Lucifer drinks blood. Without blood, he would not survive." My daddy told me and my older brothers, "These men stole things that didn't belong to them. They lost their rights. That is the reason I tell you, you can only make friends with certain children. Did you know they have been stealing? Yes, this is their blood. This morning, there is a massacre at Bamboo."

Since there were no cars in that remote area at the time, there were horses and mules tied on every corner under each tree. Then I looked to the right of the coffee vines and saw somebody I knew, Jalbert.

Jalbert was a man that we children loved very much. He would cut our hair once a month, and he was a great barber in the commune. Although he is not a member of our family, we used to see him as more than a good friend. I knew Daddy would have asked for forgiveness for Jalbert if he knew he was about to die.

"Daddy," I said softly.

Then he took a step toward Jalbert. "Here is Jalbert, Daddy! He is dead!"

My daddy backed up a little. He looked under the coffee vines and found the almost lifeless body of Jalbert, who had been marked up with knife slices everywhere on his body. Wet and dry blood was all over his body, and a large open wound was above his heart.

"Oh God! It was just last afternoon Jalbert cut the hair of all the boys for me. He cut my hair too. He is an innocent man. Why did they kill him?" Daddy began to lament. Then he turned to us, children, "Do not talk. I am taking him to the leaf doctor."

The leaf doctors used leaves for medicine when people are sick in Haiti since most of the provinces do not have regular physicians; therefore, Jalbert had to go to a doctor that used leaves as medicine.

"They probably thought he died. They will come back to retrieve the body. Please, Renold, go call Asta to help me carry Jalbert."

He could trust Asta because he is his brother although Asta is a member of the Pentecostal Church while Daddy is a Catholic and a vodou worshiper. Then came Asta, holding a white blanket, a bottle of alcohol, and a bottle of water.

"I heard them shooting all night last night. I heard mothers' lamenting all night. It was around two o'clock when the beating and shooting began. Oh God! These Macoutes have no pity for anyone." Asta wept bitterly for Jalbert.

"Oh, God of heaven, I can't believe human beings are so evil. When will you, oh God, deliver us from this hell?" These were the words of my uncle.

Daddy became agitated and irritated at his brother Asta. He looked over at him and said, "Stop your tears. Haven't you heard what's going on in Fort Dimanche? Jalbert is lucky we found his body at Fort Dimanche. They're killing them by the hundreds. They're throwing them in some ditches, piles burnt alive or dead together, or they drop them into the waters, and they disappear forever."

Fort Dimanche is a government concentration camp near the National Palace in Haiti. Usually, if the police arrest someone and they take him to Fort Dimanche, he or she will never return. They would beat him or her to death.

"If people ask you, don't say that you've seen Jalbert. If they know we saved him, they will kill us too. The officers must believe that he's dead, and they're probably coming back to retrieve the body," Daddy exclaimed.

Daddy and his brother opened the white blanket on the ground, and while they wiped young Jalbert, we three boys stood there gazing at Jalbert's cut-up and bloody body. It looked scary.

We were in tears, but I managed to ask, "Daddy, the Tontons Macoutes, are they witches too?"

Daddy was firm and persistent. "Son, we can't talk about this right now. We are trying to save Jalbert."

"Oh . . . Jalbert, se youn bon gason (Oh . . . Jalbert was a good man)," Asta cried.

They wrapped Jalbert inside that white blanket, and then they took two long pieces of wood, cut four small pieces to create a straight chair, and took him away. While we were crying and following Dad and uncle, we saw that Jalbert's blood all over the ground.

Asta said, "He won't survive. I do not think he has any more blood left."

Hearing this word from Asta, we, boys, squeezed each other's hands.

My brother, Ibra, whispered to me, "Jalbert is dead!"

Whether the life I shall live will be a long one or a short one on this earth, I shall never forget that massacre. The trail of blood I saw with my own eyes from Risqué to the river of Zorangé, from Cacola to Bamboo, and so on shall never be erased from my memory.

When we arrived, we met with a big crowd gathered to watch the event. Before the massacre started, Officer Omani stepped forward to read the names of the thieves while the crowd listened carefully. Every time they called a name, one could hear the parents' loud wails. Two officers took each victim, dragged them in the circle, and beat them. Those who died, the parents came forward later and retrieved the cadaver. Those who did not have a parent counted for the mass grave. Those who were believers of God's word knew that God would not remain silent after this massacre.

I was one of the spectators. I was only twelve years of age. I cried. I remember till this day what made me cry. I saw Norris's brother, Novas, brought into the circle by one of the police officers, and they began to beat him while his hands and feet were tied. His ten children were outside the circle, watching their father get beaten. They were terrified, but they were helpless. When I arrived at the show, I thought I was going to be the only boy watching the spectacle, but there were many other young boys watching the officers' brutal treatment of the so-called thieves.

My daddy said to us, three boys, "At least, we might save Jalbert. If he dies, we are not responsible. God knows."

Asta responded, "Oh, dear brother! I do not want to hear that we are not responsible. We allowed witches to take over Zorangé and now Tontons Macoutes. We are citizens of this commune. We participated in their religion and supported the Macoutes. As a Pentecostal Christian, my job is to tell these people to leave vodou and the evil that it does. Since I am too afraid to tell them the truth, I too washed my hands in the blood of the innocents. I should tell them that the vodou gods that they serve would make them lack conscience."

Daddy sighed and then said, "Uh . . . are you trying to preach to me, Asta? Oh, now you are pastor too. Very soon I am going to hear that you kick the pastor out and took his place. Are you a preacher? Don't preach to me, brother. I am not a Pentecostal. I will never be one. Papa Legba has done too much for me."

Asta responded, "When God wants you, you will come, and you will regret all the time that you wasted in the worship of these false gods."

And Daddy said, "Asta, let's leave this conversation alone. We are not here for discussion. We are here to save Jalbert. Let's take Jalbert to the doctor to see if we can save him."

"You are my brother. I can talk to you, allow me to tell you. You are stupid to think that Legba, the spirit of snakes that you are following, has done something for you. Let me tell you, this evil spirit will follow you from generation to generation. It is time for us to abandon our ancestors' false beliefs. Satan never leaves you. I hope you decide to accept Jesus soon like your wife and the mother of your boys. Stop being a part of these vampires. You will be just like them, and God will come to destroy you all in the commune. We should never allow our children to watch such murders."

That massacre with its trails of blood from Risqué to the river of Zorangé, from Cacola to Bamboo, and so on was instilled in my memory, in brain and heart forever. I remember the young boys—wild, innocent, and yet fated for doom so early—and the words of my father about them, "I bring you here to learn that anyone who is arrogant or stealing is not worthy to bind with us."

The officers, their wives, and their children giggled, but most of the citizens lamented in spite of the officers' opposition to express pity. The vodou priests were present, helping them decapitate some of the victims. I remember I saw two vodou priests, each took a man by each of his legs and decapitated him, and mothers fell by the river and lost consciousness.

On our way back from the massacre, I saw dogs eating a cadaver. When I looked farther, I saw three men digging a hole to bury the dead in the ground.

I called my father, "Daddy, look!"

When he saw the dogs eating the cadaver, he shot in the air. A dog ran with an arm. Then we noticed men tried to hide from us. My father pointed his gun at them. They told him the Tontons Macoutes asked them to dig the hole. We looked farther; we saw where the other bodies were buried.

It might have been Toto's blood that I saw at Bamboo. They began to beat the victims in their homes in Bamboo. I was very young when the massacre took place, but I will never forget my brother counting the number of bodies on the ground.

Lamare's body was completely decapitated. I remember him because his face looked so familiar, and I still see him in my mind's eye. The visual misery of his charred body helped me to conclude very early on that human beings can be cruel and evil to each other. The children in the area of Bamboo were unfortunate. They saw spilled blood like a carpet on the ground and brutal murders with their own eyes, and that is their nightmares as long as they live.

Adults were living in fear of the political system. Children were living in fear because the entire commune was haunted, and then came the massacre. Everyone in Oranger believed that the massacre itself was the work of the vodou gods. People were so deep in vodou that they became evil and malevolent.

I recalled the day after the massacre; a young lady named Anna came down to draw water. Everyone was looking at her and thinking of her tragedy. One of the gendarmes who came to arrest her father was staring at her. In his mind, he murmured, "Oh, such a beautiful girl. Why did I have to go and arrest her father? And now, though I love her, I can't tell her so."

Then the gendarme began to think of the event. He went in to arrest Anna's father. The mother was pleading with them not to arrest her husband. His colleague slapped the mother very hard on the face. She fell and died, and then they beat her father to death. Anna was then parentless. She came down to the pond to draw water and took care of her three young siblings.

The gendarme asked Anna, "Do you recognize me?"

Anna did not look at him; she nodded her head to say yes.

The gendarme began to cry, "I am sorry. I knew your parents. Both of them were good people."

Anna raised her head. "Why did you kill them?"

He said, "I did not kill your parents, Anna. I was doing my police duties."

Anna replied, "Well, you did not have to be a criminal for anyone. You could tell your boss that you will face your own judgment before God someday."

"I am sorry, Anna," the gendarme said.

"I accept your apology, but that's not going to help me get my parents back," Anna answered. Then Anna began to cry.

A young man, who stood there listening to the conversation, took the bucket and carried it for Anna in one hand and held Anna with the other hand. They left the gendarme standing by the water, gazing at them as they climbed up the hill.

I wish I never witnessed the massacre. If I'd known what was going to happen to my psyche, that place would have been the furthest from my mind. It was alarming.

After I watched it, I felt a sense of doom. When I think of it, I am in fear. Fear that keeps me locked in my home at night unless I am with somebody. I am afraid of the police. I am afraid of the court system. Every time I see a policeman, I think of the gendarmes in Bainet. I admit that sometimes I eat off the fear because of the litany of names that the government saw as enemies whether they were family or friends. Mention something about free speech, and you are a suspect. Casually talk about definitions of what a free society would include, and all eyes are on you, including the government. Exhilaration and stress mix together; it took nerves of steel to get through such a society—a society that was not free, not even to those who claimed to be the rulers!

I recalled Pastor Dejean and the buzz around him after he gave a sermon about the massacre. He said in one of his Sunday sermons, "I do not care if they hear me. If they want to kill me, it is fine with me. They were not out to punish people who are thieves, but they were out to kill anyone who is not like them and who is against their evil ways."

There was not an exceptional hush, not a cough, not a tapping of shoes, nor the rustling of church programs—no sounds as if the congregation was suffocating—but what was happening was gladness and fear of what Pastor Dejean had said. But he wouldn't stop.

He continued, "They are corrupt and harmful to others. There are two groups of people, up to three, that I am afraid of the most, and God himself despises them. There are those who refuse to rid themselves of their pride, turn away from their arrogance, and feel that they are secure in their spiteful willfulness, and believe they can escape from the judgment of God. The second group is those who are violent to others and say weak things from their mouths, the informer and the executioner. Third, are those who commit crimes and blame it on the poor."

Pastor Dejean continued, "The human being is the illest animal that God ever created, and the massacre at Bamboo proved it. They created apostasies among themselves. They hate their sisters and brothers. There is animosity among men everywhere. I could not believe the rich and the officers at Bamboo. They loved to shed blood. If civilization does not enlighten man, will there be another flood like in the days of Noah? I hope these officers and the rich here in Zorangé repent before God takes action against them, but it is unlikely because their hearts have become more coldhearted. I can't condemn them because they are vodou worshipers, and so they have no light. They are living in darkness, and remember, their time is short-lived."

Some of the men who survived after the massacre left the area and never returned to Bainet again. I do not know what became of them. Their families were embarrassed, their children were ashamed, but those who did it felt that they were doing the right thing then. But this evil deed remains with me forever, especially when an arrogant president is in power. He reminds me of the massacre at Bamboo. Whenever I see an arrogant judge, policeman, or lawyer, they remind me of the massacre at Bamboo.

I was explaining the massacre at Bamboo to my friend Moran, a citizen of Sri Lanka. He told me, "The massacre at Bamboo is taking place in every part of the world, and only God can stop it. And it seems that the world is going deeper into injustice because evil men get rich by doing injustice. They can raise the price of food, gas, and oil. They also can create lottery booths everywhere and take the money from the poor to finance their evil actions."

TALE 2

THE HAUNTED HOUSE

"THERE ARE MOUNTAINS behind the mountains," my father used to say.

"This world is a world of mysteries, and sometimes it can be very dark."

The mystery began when a bird flew into the house of the most notorious officer of murder and corruption, Belony. Remember him? He was the officer who came to my father's house when I was twelve and told us about the coming massacre at Bamboo.

We have met Belony before he was introduced to you, reader, in the first tale. Belony was known openly for his contempt for the poor and for being a great abuser of the poor. He was fearless as a vodou worshiper. Since January 6, 1969, he did a major vodou sacrifice for the kings. Everyone was invited to come and break the cake, and this is a ritual people celebrate in Haiti every year. They called this day, *Les Rois* (The Kings). He would go to their houses and arrest them, most of the time for nothing. He had no shame. Belony would take their lands and bed their wives.

But back to that mysterious bird that came flying to the household of Officer Belony. His wife, Madame Freda, was sitting on the balcony when she saw that a bird flew into her house. The wife got upset, for she said the bird brought misfortunes to the family. She explained to her husband, Officer Belony what happened to her.

"Belony, come here! I think we have a problem. I saw a bird enter our house. I tried to close the door to catch it, but the bird flew away. Who will die, Belony?"

"Oh, darling, why are you thinking about death? We have all the powers in the world. Who do you think can kill us? Even God himself is afraid of us, darling. We have power. We are almost immortal in this commune," Belony replied.

Freda responded, "Ah, you do not understand the power of our neighbors, especially those that are members of the little cathedral below the mountain. I am talking about my neighbors, Gomes and Manisina. You know, they both are taking communion every Sunday, but on Sunday night, they turn into all kinds of animals."

"Darling, they know if they touch our family. We are going to kill them all," replied Belony.

"Uh, I hope so. But one thing that I know, those women who go to the cathedral are very powerful. They are the evilest witches in the area. I have been observing them carefully. I don't trust them."

"I would never ask you to trust the witches around here at all. They are very powerful. They are vampires, but they are afraid of me. They know that I can kill them," replied Belony.

"Ah, before they do anything to our children and me, they will drink your blood first. If you are weak, what can you do to them?" Freda said.

A week later, on Friday morning, one of Belony's sons woke up; he found some blue powder in their courtyard. This is a powder used by the malefactors to put someone to sleep. Usually, the malefactors used this strategy to kill people, and once they die, they will become a soulless being called a zombie, a person would be dead but can be revived within a twenty-four-hour period. Once the person is buried in the cemetery, the malefactors get the person, and then they put this person to work as a slave (zombie); this person would be alive again until his time to die a natural death arrives.

"Mother," he said, "I see some blue powder on the ground."

They both took the powder and smelled it.

"Something weird just happened to us. We should never touch that powder. It is vodou!" Mrs. Belony said to her son.

The son opened his eyes wide. "That was vodou powder, Mama? Oh, Mama! What are we going to do?"

At once, they both began to sweat and also started choking. Mr. Belony knew what to do to undo the magic, but he wasn't there at the time. When he came, he tried to undo it but unsuccessfully. They did not die right away but were still affected by the powder. They became sick but should have died because, whoever touched or got exposed to the powder, was supposed to die in a short time.

That Saturday night, they never slept. They heard zombies dancing all night in their home. They were terrified. On Sunday morning, they woke up and could not get out of their house. Zombies barricaded their home with piles of stones. After great maneuvers, Belony escaped and was able to get the ailing children and his nauseated wife out of the house. Then he went to see the district police, a man named Geraldo. Though he used to be one of his best friends, Geraldo currently despised Belony for what he had done in the massacre.

When Belony complained, Geraldo said to Belony, "You got what you deserved!" He said that to Belony because some of the supposed perpetrators were his friends, and Jalbert was his cousin.

Belony almost fell. He sat on the ground and covered his face with both hands. Then without looking at Geraldo, he left.

After Belony left, he went and sat by the river. While he was there, he saw two Tontons Macoutes walking up the hill. They walked toward him by the river. They were ready to cross the river; Belony tried to walk back to his house. One of the Tontons Macoutes shot in the air.

"Where are you going, police?"

He was scared. He did not have his weapon with him. He ran. When he arrived home, his wife told him that two Tontons Macoutes came and asked for him. They told his wife to tell him that they were coming from Port-au-Prince to kill him because he beat their brother to death during the massacre. Belony got scared because he knew Tontons Macoutes from Port-au-Prince were crueler than those from Bainet. He was lucky. They did not kill his wife or the children.

His wife said, "Belony, I told you. In Haiti, nobody has power for too long. Now, Tontons Macoutes are in power. Whoever had targeted one of their family members is now in trouble. We need to leave this area now. We do not only have to deal with Tontons Macoutes, but we have to deal with the witches."

Belony stooped down and covered his face. He realized at the moment there are two forces trying to destroy him, the Macoutes and the witches. One of them will win.

Belony went back home. He took a deep breath. He murmured, "How can I save my family in the midst of these vampires?"

There was a large fig tree at his house. He went under it. He knelt down at the tree and began to pray, not to God above, but to his vodou gods. He wished one of them would hear his prayer and save him.

"Oh, Papa Legba, Ogoun Feray Papa," he prayed silently, "please save me and my family from the vampires of Zorangé."

He wanted to call the bishop of the local cathedral, but he was suspected of being one of the vampires because most of the women in that church were considered witches; the bishop must be one of them too, but he was not. Belony was fearful of what might happen to him, his wife, and his children; he called a vodou medium to come to the house.

Her name was Aunty Sòsò. She came in a dress of red, white, blue, and black. The vodou spirit (loa) called Erzilie possessed her. She sang, "Erzilie, the house isn't drizzling. Erzilie, the house isn't drizzling. If there is no water, drizzle it with lotion."

At once, she pulled a bottle of lotion and began to drizzle the house. She told Mr. Belony that his house was sold to one of the most powerful and well-known vodou priests in Haiti by the name Ozanfè. She predicted that the entire family was going to die and that she had no power to save them.

Belony did not know what to do after listening to the vodou priestess. He called his parents for help. Belony himself became ill. They were vodou worshipers. Their father brought another vodou priest. The priest began to call on Ogou for support.

Ogou Feray possessed the vodou priest by the name of Mètlakay. Mètlakay entered as he was walking left and right as if he wanted to fall to one side, but he never fell. He had on blue jeans and a red shirt, a long necklace on his neck, and he wore sunglasses though it was late afternoon. He had a straw hat on and a red handkerchief on each side of his back pocket and a straw bag around his neck.

As soon as he came in, a bottle of champagne was given to him, and then he began to talk after drinking half of the bottle of champagne.

Mètlakay told Belony that the vodou priestess Aunty Sòsò was one of the vodou priestesses who sent zombies to dance at his house that night. The urine itself was a curse that she put in the house to undo any other vodou magic Belony did, and she captured every soul in the entire house with her.

Both Officer Belony's mother and father believed in the vodou spirit. They would never drink a cup of coffee without throwing some of it on the ground for the dead, and they would never go to bed without praying to the dead to give them a good night's sleep. They believed that their vodou gods would give them victory in the end, but before the priest left, he told them Christianity is the only thing that could save the family from the evil spells and bring their souls back from vodou's jurisdiction.

Mètlakay told them, "The Pentecostal Church people are filled with a spirit that is more powerful than any other spirit. You should go to them. They will cast out all spells and heal you guys right away."

It was about a month since Aunty Sòsò urinated in the house and told Belony that she had undone everything. "Everything is going to be fine."

But Belony realized that his wife and the children were still sick. The house was filled with woes and sorrows.

One of the children said to another, "We should leave this house and go live with Pastor Dejean. I heard he has the spirit of Pentecostal too."

One morning, Belony's youngest son woke up. He felt that he was bleeding. He got up and turned on the light. He saw blood all over his bed. The blood seemed to go through the wall. He walked slowly and went to his mom and dad's room. He shook Belony.

"Daddy, I see blood." Belony asked,

"Where do you see the blood?"

Belony took his lamp and went to find out. He looked and saw blood too. It was like the blood had penetrated through the wall. He opened the door and went outside. He saw a white dog outside with its mouth on the wall. He picked up a stone and hit the dog. The dog fell. He tried to rip the dog's head. The dog changed into Gomes.

She said, "Belony Papa, don't kill me. I will pay you, and I will talk to the regiment to take away the spell from your family."

Belony was trying to make Gomes tell him what she was doing at his house. Then Belony became numb. He could no longer talk or move his hand. Belony lost consciousness. The dog left.

In the morning, Belony found himself in bed. He wasn't sure if he had dreamed it or if it was a reality. He went back outside to check. He saw the blood of his son on the wall. Belony ran to Gomes's house. Upon arrival there, he saw Gomes sitting on her porch with her nightgown on, and as he approached, she was giggling at him.

"Belony, where are you going? Are you spying on me? Or now you know how much power I have?"

Belony stood there gazing at her. Then he said to Gomes, "You can laugh. I can't afford to laugh."

Gomes began to become hysterical. She raised her nightgown, and then she turned right and left. She turned into that same dog that was outside Belony's house.

Belony began to shake. He had never seen a witch so brave and willing to let people know "I am a witch." Then Gomes changed again to normal.

Belony said to her, "Why are you doing malevolence to your neighbor?"

Gomes responded, "Why did you massacre your neighbors and send tormentors to poor families in our neighborhood?" Gomes was silent, waiting for Belony to give an answer. Belony did not respond. Gomes said, "You will regret that you were an officer. All of you who participated in the massacre will pay a heavy price for it. My son is now leaving the area. I don't know if I will see him before I die."

Belony became so anxious. He ran to his house. Once he arrived home, he called Pastor Samson to come to convert the family to Protestantism. They came on a late Sunday afternoon.

When the children heard the Protestants coming, one of the children, a boy named Geromi, was happy to meet them. He ran to meet them. When he saw them, he ran back to his house and told the parents, "I see them. I see the Protestants coming, and I will not die anymore."

The Pentecostals entered the house. They began to pray in the house. They began to speak in tongues. All the demons in the area went into hiding, including Gomes, for they believed that the Christians would expose them. They did not want people to know that they were witches because the Pentecostals were very strong and powerful. They knew how to undo the vodou spell with the blood of Jesus. In fact, those Christians did not even have to pray when they showed up in the house. Their leader, Brother Edgar, was the strongest Christian in Bainet. He was a great man of God and had a fascinating story. He tells it with such conviction and has been telling his story perpetually.

Brother Edgar suddenly became very sick one day. Everywhere he went, doctors, vodou priests, and priestesses condemned him to die with a chronic stomachache that he suffered from a poisoned food he ate when someone poisoned all the food in a wedding five years ago. Twenty people died, but Brother Edgar did not die, but he suffered from chronic stomachache. While he was in a coma, his parents called Pastor Samson, and even before the Protestants entered the house of Brother Edgar, he was healed from the poison that he ate. They could heal anyone just by singing a song.

After the prayer, people who were sick in the house were getting better. However, Belony and his wife only stayed in the church for a couple of months, then he went back to consult another vodou priest. His younger son, Jaclyn, was the only one who stayed Christian and protested against his family going back to worship vodou gods. Jacylyn was determined to keep his newly Christian faith strong. He continued to go to church, and the parents allowed him to do so.

When December arrived, everybody got ready to feed the dead. On December 25 of every year, at the house of Belony's father, Papa Yoyo had a big ceremony to offer food to the dead. Everybody came from Daraspin, Sous-Morne, Risque, and Moreau with their own food to throw around the cemetery at the premises of Daraspin. Some of the worshipers would put the food inside the tombs. The spirit would come upon my Uncle Alves. He was the most professional drummer in the whole area, and the theory was that the loas taught him how to play drums. All the daughters of Papa Yoyo received the gift of loa. At least, every December 24, the loa would mount aunts Therese, Mèmène, and Tazie. Since Belony was the only man in his family, the vodou gift or the loa never mounted him.

Usually, there was a vodou priest in charge of the service. There was a man named Seidon who was invited to perform the ceremony. Seidon showed up with a bag of many colors. He himself had stripes tied to his body and his arms; he had a bag of many colors on his shoulders and was dressed in red, white, blue, and black. He brought tortoise's blood for Belony and his family to drink. He pulled a black bottle with something that looked like blood in it and handed it to Belony.

"Take some," he instructed Belony.

Belony was afraid to drink. "What is that in the bottle?" Belony asked Papa Seidon.

"You do not have to know. Drink it," Seidon insisted again.

Since Seidon as a vodou priest was so respected, Belony drank it. Belony took some of the drink.

I saw his face change from human to a face of a cow. His face came back to normal. Seidon wanted everyone to see his power. Then Seidon started the service by making a heart with white flowers on the ground. He raised his head to the north and said, "Oh, Papa Legba, you are invited to be here now!"

Legba is one of the most important loas in Haitian vodou. He is the first called in a service so that he can open the gates to the spirit world, enabling communication with other loas. No loa dares show itself without Legba's permission. He controls the crossing over from one world to the other. Legba is also known to hold the key to the spiritual world, and this reason is identified with the Christian St. Peter.

Then he raised his head to the south and said, "Oh, Mèt Kalfou! Map tan ou Kouye a (Oh, Master Kalfou! I am waiting for you now)!"

Petro and Legba are considered intertwined or opposite; Kalfu controls the crossroads. Kalfu also controls the evil forces of the spirit world. He allows the crossing of bad luck, deliberate destruction, misfortune, and injustice. Legba controls the positive spirits of the day.

He then drew two other vèvè of Erzulie Danto. The Erzulie is a family of loas that are often associated with water (fluidity), femininity, and feminine bodies. He drew a third for Kalfu, who he believes controls the malicious spirits of the night. At once, everyone started speaking. The loa mounted Alves. Alves began to beat the drum as the women sang, "Ayi bo!" Then Kalfu descended on Alves. Even Seidon did not talk anymore. He stopped for a while. Then I learned that once Kalfu mounts a person, everyone at the service stops speaking because he allows evil loa to come to the ceremony. Kalfu is the sorcerer and is closely associated with black magic.

Then Belony said, "Hai Gede! Baron Samedi Papa. We can't do this service without you, Papa!" Ghede is dresses in black, controlling the eternal crossroad that everyone must someday pass over, the crossing from life to death. His symbol is the cross upon a tomb (*Wikipedia*).

Ghede is to the underworld or afterlife what Legba is to life. He controls access. Then Aunt Tasi was mounted by Ghede. She ran into the forest. Then where she stood behind the tree, they dug a hole and buried one of the black goats alive. Then the musicians began playing the music, and once the accordion started, the loa mounted each one of the women. The women danced from 8:00 a.m. to 8:00 p.m. and never got hungry. The only man I have ever seen to be mounted by the spirit was Uncle Alves; we all called them uncle and papa in the area. He was a very good-looking man, but once the spirit mounted him, he fell on the ground and became dirty. He ate every piece of glass that he could put his hands on. He got very drunk and became the dirtiest man that I had ever seen.

The vodou priest would throw food all over and say, "Vèvè, vèvè!"

And everyone would answer, "Vèvè, vèvè!"

The women began to dance beautifully, go up and down around the white circle created by Papa Seidon as the people used to call him.

They sang, "Papa Gédé, bèl gason. Papa Gédé, bèl gason, abye l tout an blan pou l al monte au pale (Father Gédé is a handsome man. Father Gédé is a handsome man. Dress him in white to sit on his throne)."

They brought all types of food for the loas. Every family member had offered a young black chicken to one of the dead. There were black cows, black goats, black sheep, and black pigs, and animals of three colors. They would pour the blood from the animals and drink it. There was a lot of coffee, chocolates, and sodas.

No one was allowed to eat until Papa Gédé, who was the master of the dead, finished his eating. Until this day, I never understood how they knew when Papa Gédé finished eating.

On December 25, Seidon came for the service, and after the big ceremony, he came to sleep overnight at Belony's house to also perform a ceremony for Belony and his family. As soon as he arrived, he told Belony that he was in grief. He requested to do a ceremony for Belony. He had to chase the witches that he believed would come to take the children's souls and drink their blood at night. He told Belony that one of his children does not need to participate in the ceremony.

When Belony insisted on finding out why, he told Belony that one of his children was too powerful; he could not even touch him. He asked Belony to send that child to sleep at the house of Belony's father, or his ceremony would not be successful because the youngest of Belony's sons had the power of the Pentecostals. Belony did just that. He gave them the tortoise's blood to drink, then he began to burn pieces of tires in the house, and all of them began to choke. The children were complaining but did not want Seidon to hear them.

One of the children said, "My nose is completely blocked with smoke."

Another said to Belony, "I am choking."

Belony said, "Quiet!"

The children fell asleep and did not know what had happened again, but they could have died that day.

Seidon told Belony he would give him a solution to the problem. In the morning, he asked Belony to pay him and told Belony that he called upon the loas to come and stay in the house to watch over them.

However, a few days after he left, Belony woke up; he and his family sat in the courtyard when a monster showed up. They called it *ti baca*, which means "the little monster." Ibra, one of the boys, was the first to see it, and he got sicker afterward.

The little monster was a fearful animal that had pins all over its body. It looked like a little dog, but it is not a dog because it was biped. It has fire in its eyes and mouth. Belony saw that animal many times; it had a human face and stood on its feet like a human being. At night, the animal ate every dog Belony brought to the house. Belony had a dog by the name of Noula. When the animal tried to eat the dog, the dog went inside the house; Belony kicked Noula out due to fear that the monster might enter the house to find the dog, and in the morning, he only found pieces of the dog's bones.

They all became fearful of the house. The animal went under children's legs and made them very sick. Later on, Belony learned that the monster appeared after a big ceremony that his dad had ten years ago. He had seven animals alive. Then they became evil to haunt the family. The animal didn't bite them physically, but it scared them to death, and wherever it touched someone, it bled because of the pins on the animal's body. Whenever the animal came to the house, something tragic happened. A cow, a goat, a horse, or a pig would die. And whoever had seen it first would get very sick.

Every night, demons came to dance in their courtyard. They sang, played music, and made noises in the courtyard. Belony recalled some day when the witches called him by name to come out. He never went out. But every time they showed up, Belony lost consciousness and would have a seizure.

Six months after the vodou priest's visits, one of the sons died. Brenis was the first to die on a Thursday since he was also the first to find the powder. Then the night after his funeral, a vodou band brought him to the house. They confronted Belony in the courtyard. They told him, "Father, you are the one who caused us to die because you killed so many innocent men in the massacre of Bamboo. You accused them for no reason. We are all going to lose our lives one by one due to your injustice."

Then Belony yelled till he had a seizure and lost consciousness. Second, Belony's wife died the following Thursday; she had also touched and smelled the powder. The following Thursday, Belony's mother-in-law, who used to come to the house, died, and then followed his daughter Jester's death. Right after the death of Jester, Belony left the house because it was haunted; however, he died three months later. There was only one child left of Belony, Jaclyn. The rest all died with their parents. That took my complete attention since I was a young kid.

Jaclyn left vodou to become a Christian. God gave him his power, and since then, he swore not to ever believe in anything but the God who created the heavens and the earth.

"Religions can enlighten men, but religions can make men become evil, dumb, and savage if they do not embrace the true religion," said Jaclyn.

Result of the Massacre

Three years after the massacre, Belony and his family were wiped out. And one of the men, Mr. Richard, who committed the crimes against those poor men, committed suicide. Before his death, that night, we saw a star fall in the sea from the sky. We all heard the noise and saw it falling into the sea.

My father said, "A strong man is going to fall."

We did not know who, but it was true what my father said, "The stars in the sky mean something. They are our shadows in the heavens. When we do badly to earth, right before we die, they fall in the sea, and that is where they remain until Judgment Day."

One month after that, Monsieur Richard died. The entire area was mourning while the poor were rejoicing, but it was just a beginning. Most of the police officers died one after the other, and never again a massacre such as that ever took place at Bamboo. Most people thought God took revenge for Abel and the other innocent men that lost their lives in Bamboo.

As Monsieur Jeremie said, "You watch any country, city, or town that does evil to the poor will pay for it. God will bring destruction upon them and their properties."

Three and half years after the massacre, the river came down and took one of the officers to the sea. They have yet to find the body to this day. The river also took horses, goats, pigs, and everything the rich owned in the area, including their lands. It was the first time that we saw the river come down so strongly in July. None of us expected to see so much of the wealth of the rich destroyed by the water; God punished them for being so cruel to the poor.

After the disaster, Pastor Samson called for a rally at the Bamboo marketplace. He preached then, "God does not take time to punish evil. When he decides, it will happen on his own time."

"Yes!" he said, "I love to see the God of love take revenge. No one can fight him back."

After Pastor Samson's sermon, Brother Edgar stood up. "Ladies and gentlemen, brothers and sisters, how long do you want to continue to stay under the punishment of God?"

Everyone turned to look at him. He also turned and looked at everyone around the marketplace.

"You who are here today, listen to me. The same God that Peter preached in the book of Acts, chapter 2, is the same God Pastor Samson preached to you today. On the day of Pentecostal, people heard Peter's sermon, and they repented. Today, God's judgment is upon you. If you do not repent, God will continue to send his judgment, but if you repent, God will send his Holy Spirit upon you as he did on the day of Pentecost. To repent, you do not have to make sacrifices as you have done every year to Erzulie and Legba. You only need to accept Jesus Christ as your Lord, ask him to forgive your sins, and he will forgive you not only of the sins you have now in your life but of the past sins as well. None of us can say we are innocent. Each one of us has a family member who is involved in vodou worship. Each one of us has a family member who is a witch.

"Jesus came to this earth to perform wonders, but they killed him, and the Israelites did not stay unpunished. They were taken away by other nations as slaves, but today, you may not have any other nations that will take you as slaves, but you are the slaves of vodou, and that is the reason our chiefs have no respect for us. They killed our children, brother, and fathers. If you want your respect back as a people, accept Jesus Christ as your personal savior, and you will be set free."

Edgar continued, "I feel that God wants to raise some of you as his witnesses today. I feel that there are some of you God wants to set free."

Then one person raised his hand. "What should we do, Brother Edgar?"

Brother Edgar responded, "Accept Christ as your personal savior, and you will be saved."

Then the congregation began to sing this song:

> Just as I am, without one plea,
> But that Thy blood was shed for me,
> And that Thou bidd'st me come to Thee,
> O Lamb of God, I come, I come.

Then people began to go on their knees. When they began to sing:

> Just as I am, and waiting not
> To rid my soul of one dark blot,
> To Thee whose blood can cleanse each spot,
> O Lamb of God, I come, I come.
> More people came forward. After the third verse:
> Just as I am, tho' tossed about
> With many a conflict, many a doubt,
> Fighting and fears within, without,
> O Lamb of God, I come, I come.

By the time that the fourth verse ended, I looked up, and some of the sisters from Notre Dame of Bas de Gandou came to accept Christ, some coming from Daraspin, Sous-Morne, Risque, and Moreau. They came and went down on their knees to accept Jesus Christ as their personal savior. There was no more space for people to kneel. I heard a woman say, "Pentecostals are taking over Bainet. The Catholic churches around here will be closed."

> Just as I am, poor, wretched, blind—
> Sight, riches, healing of the mind,
> Yea, all I need in Thee to find—
> O Lamb of God, I come, I come.

Brother Edgar said, "Let us read the fifth verse. They read as following:

> Just as I am, Thou wilt receive,
> Wilt welcome, pardon, cleanse, relieve,
> Because Thy promise I believe,
> O Lamb of God, I come! I come!

I heard people lamenting. I saw Father Gerald, the priest of the Bar de Gandou Cathedral, come forward. He knelt and accepted Christ as his personal savior. There was a revival in Bainet.

TALE 3

THE POWER OF WITCHES IN RISQUÉ

WHEN DECEMBER ARRIVED, each one of us thought we were going to be the next one to die. December was the darkest month for children. I remember staying fully awake for the entire month at night and slept during the day, and I was not alone.

Every day, a child used to die. I remember I was ten years old then around December 1967.

I asked my father, "Dad, who is going to die next week, Brenis or me?"

My father responded, "Neither you nor Brenis will die, Mario. Papa Ogou and Agwe are watching over you. Your mom and I just fed all the loa. They are not hungry. We fed Agwe, La Sirène, and Baron Samedi. And his wife, Manman Brijit, came. She danced, and she was very pleased with the ceremony."

And I responded, "Daddy, I do not believe Ogou or Agwe are alive. What about all the other children who are dying? I have seen their parents making sacrifices to the loa for them every year."

"Oh, son, don't talk about the dead like this." My father looked at me in disbelief, and then he said, "They are our protectors."

I never believed my father then because children were dying all around me. It was a social and psychological disaster. I never understood why December was the month when most children used to die until I asked my parents, and they told me it was because December was the month for the witches to pay their dues.

Women were also some of the targets. For some reason, men were spared from that epidemic. As a child, if one went to some place and a woman scratched his or her hand or told him or her something unusual, one must tell his or her parents right away so that the parents could run to the witch's house and tell her, "If anything happens to my child, you are responsible."

Some parents had to bring the witches to justice or the child would die.

The witches with money would pay a police chief to protect her. The money would be shared with the officers. When the witch arrived in court, the judge would make the parents pay for the accused witch if there was no evidence, and usually, the children would die, and one would not be able to take the witch to court anymore.

Our parents asked us to never eat food from any stranger. In fact, if anyone gave me something to eat, I had to inform my dad about it. I learned that everyone in the area could have been one of the witches. Every woman was considered a witch, and most of the time, it was true. I used to wonder why the women were sleeping during the day. I could not believe some of my neighbors who were belonged to the Zorangé Cathedral. I knew it was a Catholic church because I used to see the sisters wear long white-and-black robes and wear nice bandanas. Those women were fasting every day. They used to go from house to house to pray until the bishop got sick. We learned that his sister and some of the witches put spells on him so that they could devour him in the next December's ceremony. Unfortunately for the witches in that local church, the bishop called the Pentecostal church to come and pray with him. The members from that church were filled with the Holy Spirit.

One of the women from the Pentecostal church revealed to the bishop that some of his church members were involved in witchcraft and that they put spells on him to die for the next December's rite. The Pentecostals prayed for him and freed him from the vodou spell.

Gomes, Phanise, Phasile, Chimène, Clotide, and Rena, to name a few, slept during the day and went hunting at night. My father used to tell us to be careful with our closest neighbor, Gomes. She put to sleep many of her grandchildren and others around the area of Zorangé.

"Children, never say bad things to anyone," my parents used to say. They believed that if a child wasn't wise, he was a likely target for the witches, but I never recall being too wise with them, especially Obier and Masina. I wasn't going around making trouble with the witches, but when I learned that one of the women was a witch, I didn't deal with her. One day, my father saw Gomes in front of our house at night. My father ran behind her. She became a dog and ran away.

My father followed her to her home, and in the morning, my father went and told her, "Don't do it again." My father said, "You should stay away from my house, or I will cut your head off."

She said to my father, "Please don't tell anybody, but I will never go back to your house again."

In that same week, Toro saw a flying human in the middle of the road at Tikalbas around two o'clock in the morning. Toro did not know exactly whom he encountered. He saw a young woman flying with her legs straight behind under her tail, like an eagle, and her arms under her wings, flying. Toro performed a prayer that his father taught him before this sorcerer turned him into a horse. Then he threw a stone at her. She tried to fly farther, but she fell on the ground somewhere near her home. She forced herself up and entered her home.

In the morning, one of her grandchildren woke up and told her father, "Daddy, I see blood."

The father said, "Where do you see the blood?"

He pointed, and the father looked and saw a trail of blood. He followed the trail of blood from his house to a place called Tikalbas, near the river of Oranger. Then he learned that Toro, who was known as a magician and vodou drummer in the area of Oranger, stoned his mother-in-law during the night. As Toro was trying to pass under the large *mombin* tree, she shook the tree on him and scared him at midnight.

He went and saw his mother-in-law under a blanket filled with blood. Many people testified that they heard Rena lamenting until she arrived home. Early in the morning, we learned that Rena woke up with a huge hole on her left side. Toro spread the news that he found the sorcerer at Tikalbas. When he stoned the sorcerer, it was Rena, my brother's godmother, who died a few weeks later. She never told anyone what happened to her, but Toro spread the news.

The witches passed down their witches' gifts from generation to generation. They only gave it to the female children they loved or to their good female friends but mostly to women because it was difficult to pass it down to boys. As a vodou witch says, "It takes forever to train boys."

Most men were unable to become witches. I learned from some of the witches that it was very hard to pass the gift to men and boys because men could not fly. Also, it took an eternity for a man to become a witch, but three days for a woman or a girl.

One day, I went to Mrs. Gomes's place. She sat in front of me on the balcony, and I looked right into her eyes. I thought I did that due to fear that she might scratch my hand or force me to eat some type of food.

She said, "Don't look at me in the eyes!"

I continued looking at her in the eyes. She spat in my face. "Don't look at me, Toro! You are a witch!"

She referred to me as Toro because she wanted to do something to me, but she was unable to do so due to her fear for my father. She saw me as someone with the power of Toro, who killed Rena.

I said to her, "You witch. You can't do anything to me."

She answered, "Who told you I am a witch?"

"My father," I answered.

She went, "Oh . . . ah . . . oh . . . ha . . . Your father said that?"

She tried to grab me. I ran. My father was standing nearby, but neither Gomes nor I saw him.

He said to her, "What were you going to do to him?" She did not answer. He repeated again, "Tell me what you were going to do to him."

Gomes answered, "Nothing."

"You said nothing," my father said, "but touch him, and you will see what I will do to you."

Later on, my father told me that I did the right thing to tell her that she was a witch. By telling Gomes that she was a witch, it would disable her from putting a spell on me.

I knew something was going on when I saw Mrs. Asthma holding her ear. I asked, "Are you okay, Aunty Asthma?"

"No," she answered. "I heard gunshots in my ear. I heard horses running, pigs squealing, and cows mooing."

I said, "Oh, Lord, what is going on with her?"

As I was standing there, Mrs. Asthma told me, "Did you just see what happened?"

I answered, "No."

"She said someone just gave me blood to drink and told me to let go. I am not here right now. I am already at Ozanfè's."

I never knew that Mrs. Asthma was one of the witches at Risqué. My father told me two weeks ago that they found some remedy for the vampires. I murmured, "There is no way Mrs. Asthma could be one of the witches. I am with that woman every day since I was a child."

And at that time, I was in my teen years when I found out that she was a witch. She could have scratched my hands. I could have died long ago. Maybe she ate some of my sisters' and brothers' meat. One of my uncle's daughters, Sonia, and his son, Simon, had just passed away one after the other, three days apart.

I stood there in fear. I was then fourteen years of age, but I knew everything about the witches. I knew the kind of questions to ask them to make them talk to me. I knew what to tell them to make them afraid of me. If they try to get me, my father had told me how to defend myself.

All my hair stood on end. I said to Mrs. Asthma, "I think I can save you, but tell me the truth. Are you a witch? Have you eaten any human meat?"

She turned to look at me while she was in the bed. She opened her eyes very wide when she heard that I can save her from death. She only had two more hours to live. I just came from the river of Zorangé. There I learned that one of the witches scratched the children days before, causing their deaths when the mother took him to the cathedral. After he came back from confession, he was very sick.

Another neighbor told my uncle, "Make sure that you go to a vodou priest to save your children. Now, most of the witches go to church to hide. It is easier for them to scratch children there."

My uncle went to a vodou priest before he buried his daughter. The vodou priest gave him some secret to kill the witches. In a vodou world, revenge never ends.

Mrs. Asthma turned and said to me, "I killed both Simon and Sonia. I still have more meat."

I slapped Mrs. Asthma on the face and said, "You ate my niece and nephew?" Then I ran.

The night of the funeral, I was talking to Mrs. Asthma. We used to call her Aunt Marie; she was in good spirit. The next afternoon, I went to her home, and she was sick. I ran to my grandpa to inform him that Aunt Marie was sick, but I pretended that I did not know what was going on.

My grandpa said, "Is she complaining about an ear infection? Or did she tell you that she heard animals in her ear?"

I said, "Yes, but how do you know?"

He said, "She might be one of the witches, and if she is, she will die at eight tonight."

"It is six o'clock, Grandpa," I responded.

"Yes, she has two hours to live," Grandpa replied.

After the death of Sonia, Aunt Marie died at 8:00 p.m. the following day. All who ate Sonia's body with Aunt Marie began to die. For some reason, nobody in the area knew that Aunt Marie was a witch because we knew witches in the area by name, but Aunt Marie's name was never mentioned. The news went fast that the neighbors found the remedy for the witches, and that stopped the frequent deaths of children and women in the area just for a while.

About five years later, Gomes died. I happened to be there for the funeral. The woman who was hired to shower the cadaver asked Gomes's son, Laval, to pull the bed away from the cadaver. As soon as Laval moved the bed, they looked and saw places where holes were dug in the house. The woman began to check, and she was stunned to find bones of children's legs, heads, toes, and arms under her bed. When they searched the house, they could see that she ate hundreds of children, men, and women. During her funeral, people could no longer cry for her because of the evil she had committed before her death. People knew that Gomes was one of the witches in Zorangé, but no one knew that she was such a powerful vampire in Risqué.

As of today, I still have complete fear for Zorangé, Bainet, and the town of Risqué. The last I heard, there are still witches in Risqué as in most places in that country. Vodou continues to be a daily practice, and demons are continuing to exercise their powers. Only the vigilante work of the Gospel of Jesus Christ can penetrate into the hearts of these evil spirits and save those who want to be rescued from the dominant forces of vodou.

TALE 4

THE POWER OF VODOU

B OTH JACQUES'S PARENTS lost their lives in October 1967. His house was haunted. He knew that his father went to every vodou priest in the area; no one was able to help him. He lost his two brothers and a sister. He was the only one left, and then he became very ill. Every night, the *bizango* group came to dance at his house. A *bizango* society is a secret society that exists in vodou culture. The belief is that they kill somebody by magical means, and after a period of time, they raise that person to perform various types of work as a zombie. This society is feared in Haiti because of its evil deeds and its strong military style.

He never slept at night. He called Pastor Jean-Baptiste, who came and converted him into the Protestant faith. On the same night, he did not hear the bizangos. He slept freely. He then realized that Jesus of Nazareth is a genuine savior and the only remedy for Haiti. His health improved right away and that gave him peace of mind. He became a testimony to what God can do in the local Pentecostal church.

On Sunday afternoons, Pastor Jean-Baptiste always showed up in the area to preach. He said, "God is calling you to come to him. If you come and leave vodou, leave witchcraft, God will prepare a place for you in heaven where you will live with him, his son, Jesus, and the Holy Spirit for all eternity. But those who refused to believe, they will be doomed, and they will receive eternal punishment from God together with Satan forever."

Pastor Jean-Baptist continued, "God is here to save you from vodou. He wants to take the place of your vodou gods who are taking away our liberty to be who God created us to be. You must repent now and save yourself and your children, for his grace is the source of salvation for all. God's judgment is nearer to you than before. Take him now to save yourself and your children, and if you do not, the demon's spirit will be so strong in the world. It will force you to give yourself to demonic powers and sacrifice your own children."

After Pastor Jean-Baptiste preached, one of the officers came to visit him. He said to Pastor Jean-Baptiste, "If you do not stop your nonsense gospel about all of us to leave vodou, we will kill you before you continue to disrespect us." The chief continued, "If I don't shoot you, I know the vodou priests and priestesses will do the job."

Pastor Jean-Baptiste replied, "I know. I am fighting against two evil forces, the Tontons Macoutes and the vodou worshipers, but what's in me is stronger than what's in them." He showed no fear for the Tontons Macoutes.

My experience is that they are not only offering animals for sacrifices but also human sacrifices are taking place in my country, Haiti. When I was a kid, I used to watch animal sacrifices, but that never affected me until one day I was assisting a vodou ritual in December. They sacrificed many black cows, black goats, black pigs, and black chickens. Then Mr. Lafarge, the master of the ceremony went into a room to talk to one of the witches who were dancing on fire. I remember watching her dancing on fire as they played drums and sang, "Mete dife nan bouda Marinèt, Marinèt pa genyen byen pou l wè, mete dife (Set fire in Marinèt's behind. Marinèt has nothing good in her. Set fire)."

She told him that she wanted to talk to him separately because she had something secret to share with him, and I overheard them. They went behind a tree, and as a child, I went behind them and hid on the other side of the tree because I wanted to hear the secret. I heard the woman say to him, "I already have three children ready for you whenever you are ready for the sacrifice. I already fried their souls and put their blood in bottles."

Mr. Lafage sighed. "Oh! You cause me a lot of trouble."

"Why do you sigh? You do not need my children?"

"Oh! Thank you," Mr. Lafage answered. "I need every soul I can get. It is nice of you to think of me, but I have been fascinated with the number of souls I received since I got here a week ago. But a woman in your position, I am sure you know my wife does not come with me. You are going to sleep with me tonight."

"Oh! I can't believe you say that, but of course!"

I never understood what she meant; I went and explained to my father what I heard. He said to me, "Be careful, for heaven's sake. You should never go over there. Since the ceremony started, Lafage told me that he collected fifty children's souls. I am quite certain that, at the end of the ceremony, they will sacrifice many children that they will raise from the dead. I am sure that Ismeta, who died last week, will be part of the sacrifice, and I am going to find out who killed her."

My father said again, "Many children you see by the river are already dead. Their souls had already been judged and condensed by the bizangos. You might see them alive, taking swimming lessons with you in the river, but they had already died."

The servant just brought the noon meal to my father and me. I did not touch the meal. I was thinking of the witches, and then I began to see every child who died in Risqué. I remembered them. I raised my eyes and looked at my dad. I was crying. I said, "When I grow up, Daddy, I will have the power of Jesus and heal all the demons. I think they are sick, Daddy."

My father looked at me and said, "Son, you are right. They are sick but don't try to play with the demons. They will kill you."

"Daddy, they have no power over me."

There was a long moment of silence during which I was lamenting. My father said, "When you see that a child has died, somebody probably fried his or her spirit years before his death."

One example of what my father told me was when Madeleine was sick once. We all went to see her. When we arrived, we saw her very sick in her pink nightgown, lying on the bed. Lano, her son, had only one child, and the child was also ill. His name was Ti Lano.

Lano went to a vodou priest, who told him that his dying mother was the one that was doing wrong to his son. Lano came back to face his mother with the situation in their house, right in our presence.

The mother said to Lano, "What did you want me to do? I owed a lot of meat to the regiment. I had to pay them somehow."

Lano asked Madeleine in our presence while she was lying on the bed, "Mother, please save my son for me. I love him. And you know that when you die, I have nobody else. If he dies, I will die too."

Madeleine replied to Lano, "I already fried his soul. Go to the kitchen, and the oil you see in the bottle behind the door is your son's soul."

Madeleine died three days later, and her son also died on the same day.

I recalled saying to my father, "I still can't understand these mysteries of vodou, witchcraft, magic. How do people turn to all these things? Science does not prove all these things."

My father responded, "Science does not fully develop to recognize every mystery that exists, and it will never be able to understand the world completely. The power of vodou in Haiti is beyond belief to people who never heard of it or seen it, but for me, vodou is very powerful. Vodou becomes a religion in which both human sacrifices, as well as animal sacrifices, are taking place.

Vodou is a powerful witchcraft religion that turns people into zombies. Some of the vodou priests have the power to turn into animals to go out at night to eat reptiles and drink the blood of weaker animals. One thing I can tell you, I have lived this type of life for sixty-five years. My grandparents, as well as my parents, have lived it.

The first time I saw an animal sacrifice, I shook through the entire ceremony. They put the knife under the chicken's neck, and while the chicken was still alive, they were passing the blood to each other, and they drank it. They took the chicken, put a knife under the chicken's neck, and put a cup or bowl under it to draw the blood then twisted its neck. The beheading of the chicken was heartbreaking to me, but the most upsetting part of it for me was the passing of the blood from person to person.

My father told me, "Be careful. Most of these women are witches. They drink real human blood."

I saw each one who took the blood, drank, and passed it to the others who possessed the loa. Then they sprinkled the rest on the attendees. I remember that day I could not handle the situation alone. I went to God. The Holy Spirit told me to go and talk to Lafage, and I did just that. I went to the ceremony, and I said to him, "How are you, Mr. Lafage?"

"Who are you?" he asked me.

"I am a Christian," I said.

"That's not important to me at this time. Don't you see what I am doing? Who are your parents?" he replied.

"Mr. Lafage, my parents are Christ Jesus who died on the cross to give me eternal life." I continued, "Of course, I see what you are doing, Mr. Lafage, but I think the reason why you are doing it is because you are in the dark. I want to bring light into your life."

"I give you two minutes to leave this place, or you will stay here as a goat," Mr. Lafage told me.

"I guess you are mistaken. I am a child of God. I am here to offer you Jesus. If you accept him, he will forgive you even if you have the souls of the children in your possessions as long as you are willing to leave your vodou to come to God. And if you do not call me to pray with you before you leave with all these zombies to go back to Port-au-Prince, you will die on your way to Port-au-Prince. I also want to let you know my soul is secure in God's kingdom, and you cannot do anything to me in Jesus's name." Then I left.

While I was leaving, I heard him say, "I will not leave without your zombie."

Later that afternoon, I was sitting on the balcony with my dad, and I saw Mr. Lafage coming toward my dad, and I knew he was going to stop at our house. He arrived at the fence; he stood there for a minute. He saw us looking at him.

My father saluted him and said, "Mr. Lafage, I have no words to express my gratitude for the work you do. Many of us in the habitation were thinking about how we were going to feed the dead this year. You came, and everyone is satisfied." Then my father introduced me. "Mr. Lafage, this is my son, Mario. He is the pastor in the family. You know, no matter what I taught him, he wants to follow Jesus. That's his choice."

He tried to shake my hand.

I pulled my hand away from him, and I said, "Good morning, Mr. Lafage." And I smiled.

He looked at me with a grim face. He did not answer. Then he looked at my father and said, "I learned this afternoon that this boy is your son. He is impertinent. He came to the ceremony to insult me. Not only did he try to preach to me his Jesus, but he told me I will not leave this place with the zombies."

My father turned and looked at me with a grimmer face than that of Mr. Lafage's. "Did you dare do that?" A nervous and angry father looked at his son. "You need to ask Mr. Lafage for forgiveness. Don't you know Mr. Lafage can take your zombie right now? This is a very powerful man. Your Jesus can't save you from this man."

Mr. Lafage shook my father's hand. Then he clapped both his hands. "You are a good father, Mr. Nicolas."

Then both men stopped looking at me to make my move.

I said, "Mr. Lafage, I am happy that you learned where I live to come here and talk to my father about rudeness, but I have a father that is greater than my father. His name is Jesus. He was the one who sent me to you. You can meet with him now if you wish by kneeling before me. I will pray for you to accept him as your personal savior, and then you will have a relationship with him. You can complain to him when you wish. I have no regrets that I spoke to you the way I did. You people are committing the most barbaric acts here in Bainet. So many children lost their lives, and I learned that you and others killed these human beings by means of vodou, but the God of mercy can save you."

Then Mr. Lafage did not say a word; he took off. My father ran after him.

"Please, Mr. Lafage, children these days are bad. Forgive him for me, Mr. Lafage."

"If you want his zombie back, you must reach me before I leave for Port-au-Prince," he replied to my father.

My father ran back to me. "Ah, you hear it? He already took your zombie. He probably came here to forgive you, and you messed up. I don't care anymore if you die. I told you to give up on your church, and you refused."

I smiled and said, "Father, my zombie is not with him. He has no power over me. I am a Christian."

"I hope so" my father replied.

Two weeks later, he completed the ceremony and went back to Port-au-Prince. The car he was driving turned upside down; he and his two vodou priests with him were killed. I recalled my father was working in the field when he heard the news that Mr. Lafage had an unfortunate fatal accident. I was taking a nap when Dad knocked on my door.

"Mario, do you want to hear this?"

"What is it, Dad?"

"Lafage has died."

I thought, *My God*. And said to him, "How?"

"He died in a car accident while he was on his way to Port-au-Prince. Two other vodou priests were with him. They were accompanying him to complete the ceremony. All were killed when a truck hit their car. Son, I believe that Jesus is alive."

TALE 5

VODOU AND THE RICH

THERE IS A belief in Haiti that many of the rich, or those with money, belong to some bizango societies or the Tontons Macoutes. For some, this was a myth, but many times, it was true. Here is a story I am going to share with you that took place around the years 1969 and 1970. It begins with a woman named Yvrose Bourgin.

Yvrose was a tiny woman with large eyes and long black hair that seemed similar to that of an Indian woman. She was the most attractive woman in the commune of Bainet. She was elegant. She paid an enormous price for her beauty.

Rich men from everywhere came to the area to look for her, but most of those men were vodou worshipers. Most of them went to vodou priests to gain their wealth and powers. If a woman married or had an affair with one of them, one took a big chance.

There was a man who lived up the hill by the name of Fabien Cadet; he was a married man, but he proposed to have an affair with Yvrose. You know, the people at Zorangé have a reputation for gossiping. They have a hard time keeping their mouths shut. Once they saw Mr. Fabien enter inside Yvrose's fence, they knew that she was trapped.

"Why would she accept to have an affair with the devil?" the people wondered.

He proposed to her long ago, but she did not accept him. This time, he came with magic and put her to sleep, and then she accepted. Mr. Fabien's wife told Yvrose that any child that she carried for her husband would be a little vampire.

She got pregnant. This baby moved in her stomach sometimes as a snake, other times as a human, sometimes as an animal with four legs (quadruped). She told her parents about the signs. They went to consult a vodou medium as was the culture of most Haitians. The vodou priest told the parents that she carried a demon in her stomach because the man who put a seed in her is a demon and his wife is a magician.

Her father told her that she would bear a son, but he would be a demon. She was unhappy, but she didn't believe it. The child was born; he looked just like his father. He was a very handsome boy, and Yvrose named him Fabrice. The baby was normal when he was born. He did everything, including walking, talking, even going to school in his third year. However, it was when he went to school that the demonic spirit began to manifest in him.

One day, Fabrice went to school, and then he pushed another child so hard down the stairs that he suffered a tragic fate. They transferred Fabrice into another school. Two years later, in the middle of the class, he pulled a snake from his little multicolored bag that his dad had purchased for him. All the children were frightened when they saw the snake because they thought it would bite them. Fabrice paraded the snake around the room with a sweet, sick smile on his face, dementedly laughing. The teacher naturally tried to pull the snake from him but was bitten. The teacher then became dumb and was unable to speak because he could not talk after the snakebite. However, he was able to speak two weeks after the incident. He testified that he saw the child turn into a sixty-five-year-old man. Four teachers were in the class. They did not get a chance to catch the snake until it disappeared. Right away, one of the teachers went to call a vodou priest in the area to see if he could save his coworker; the vodou priest predicted the death of the teacher, for poison had set in and was not going to leave the teacher. He also asked them to remove Fabrice from the school right away, or his power would affect them all.

They took him out of the school, but he appeared every morning to school in some different forms. Parents had to withdraw their children from the school, and the school director died a few years later. The school became a haunted place.

Another day, Fabrice went to the school, and the mother knew that there was no one in the house but her and her mother. Her mother said, "Yvrose, I will be back. I am headed to the river to draw some water."

After the mother left, Yvrose heard something moving around the house. "Who is there?" she asked.

She looked right and left. Then she began to move slowly to find the location of the noise. She did not see anything.

"Who is there?" she asked.

She opened the curtain from the living room to the dining room very quickly. There was nothing there. She opened the curtain to her bedroom; there was nothing there, but she tripped on something. She tried to yell; she lost her voice. She tried to call her mother, but her mouth was full of water. She tried to use her hands; both hands got heavy. Her feet got heavy. She fell to the ground. She looked up; she saw an old man sitting in the dining room with a snake around his neck, and a gigantic snake was moving toward her.

When the mother arrived, she saw Yvrose unconscious on the ground. She saw the snake moving toward her.

"What is happening!" the mother exclaimed.

She saw Fabrice sitting on one of the chairs with his entire hair turning gray and a snake around his neck. The mother began to become numb. There was a cross that her grandpa planted a long time ago in the yard; she ran out and pulled it and hit Fabrice on the head. At once, Yvrose woke up, and Fabrice became normal; both snakes disappeared.

Later on, a vodou priest told Yvrose and his mother to put crosses all over the house because the spirit fears crosses. The family became distressed, but Fabien, the father, knew exactly what his wife did but did not want to do anything to help Yvrose. His wife warned him that if he did anything, she would kill him because she was an experienced sorcerer in the area. But he warned Yvrose not to try to kill Fabrice.

He said to Yvrose, "If Fabrice realizes that you are trying to kill him, everyone in the house would be victimized."

Yvrose received many visits from all sorts of snakes on a daily basis. Until one day, there was a preacher in the mountain called Frère Sauveur (Brother Sauveur).

The preacher went to the river to draw water; although he heard about Fabrice and the troubles that he created in the entire area, he never expected to encounter him. He was the pastor of a local church in Cakor. He was known for his power of healing and chasing evil spirits in the commune. Whenever someone got sick in the commune, he would be called to heal the person. For example, there was a woman in the area by the name of Asefi. There used to be this vodou spirit that manifested in her. Whenever the spirit came upon her, she had to drink two gallons of gas and two bars of soap, or the spirit would kill her. Her parents were so poor; sometimes, they did not have the money to buy the two gallons of gas and the soaps. Therefore, they had to put her in chains, or the demon spirit would run away with her and make her harm herself.

One day, the demon spirit came upon her. The parents tied her up and called Frère Sauveur. As soon as he arrived, the demon said, "Where are you going, man of God? I know you."

Frère Sauveur pulled out his Bible and said to the demon, "In the name of Jesus, I bind and throw you in the pit of hell forever. Leave this woman."

He whacked Asefi very hard on her head with the Bible, and before he even prayed, the demon spirit left this woman forever. She soon became the wife of a pastor in Bainet.

Brother Sauveur saw Fabrice soaking in the water, taking a bath. "What are you doing here alone?" he asked Fabrice without knowing who Fabrice was. "You are a child! Where are your parents? Who allowed you to come to the river alone at this time? I am sure they know how dangerous this river can be. I can't believe that any responsible parent would leave a child in the river alone at this time."

It was kind of dark; many adults were still walking along the river, but the child was on a corner by himself.

In a few minutes, Sauveur did not see Fabrice. "Where is he?" Sauveur asked himself. Then Sauveur felt something pulling both his feet into the deep water. He tried to pull back; he was numb. He began to lose control of his tongue. Then there were two men who were talking on the other side of the river who saw Sauveur talking to the boy; they tried to get to the other side of the river to ask Sauveur to run, but the water was so deep, they had to walk a long way to find an area where the water was less deep for them to cross.

Sauveur said, "In the name of Jesus!"

The snake released him, but the snake then raised its head to see what Sauveur was doing. Sauveur was able to reach his machete, took the snake on the head, cut the snake into two pieces. At once, the snake tried to grab Sauveur into the river. Sauveur said to Fabrice, "In the name of Jesus, I destroy you."

Two other men saw and heard what was taking place between Sauveur and Fabrice; they ran to the water to ask him to run away. When Sauveur cut the snake into small pieces, people ran down with matches and gas. They set fire to the snake and burned it.

After that dramatic incident, no one ever saw Fabrice or dreamed of him. This was too fantastic to believe, and some people cherished it because they had found the source of the power to repel demons of all kinds, Jesus Christ as practiced by the Protestants. And the entire area of Zorangé knew that. One either had to be a Christian or a demon in the area. The vodou worshipers never wanted to deal with the Protestants. They thought the Protestants had too much power. They could not understand why the Protestants were so powerful.

But one of the Tontons Macoutes came to Brother Sauveur and said to him, "Who do you think you are, a savior? I heard now you Protestants reveal every secret in this society, and you have the power to kill, okay? But if I receive orders to arrest you, you will not make it to jail. I will kill you at once."

Brother Sauveur answered, "You can do whatever you wish, but make sure that your order is coming from God because I know one authentic power, the God of heaven."

TALE 6

LIANA AND THE RICH MAN

LIANA IS A beautiful woman in Coraille. Her parents, Mr. and Mrs. François, were well-known in the region of Coraille, commune of Bainet, Lower Gandou.

One day, Liana sat by the river; she saw an elegant, rich, and well-known man gazing at her. She cast a look at him also; then since she was alone in the river, she felt fearful, put her clothes on, and ran to her house. The man followed her. When he arrived, he introduced himself to Liana's parents. They were delighted to meet him. Liana's parents knew both of Robert's parents. His father's name was Al; his mother's name was Emily. The father is an officer in the area and also a well-known bizango master. He took his secret army out so early every Thursday night. The citizens in the area knew not to go out after eight o'clock in the evening due to the fear of getting caught by the bizango. The mother is a successful store owner who was well-founded in vodou. She was possessed by many loa, including Ayida-Wedo and Erzilie Freda.

Robert went in and told her that he loved her. Liana asked him to talk to her parents because she was still living in their home. The man went to Liana's parents and asked them for her hand in marriage.

Liana married Mr. Robert Pierre. They had two boys and a girl. She named the boys Frank and Kerry, and the daughter was named Bethany.

Frank died when he was six years of age. There were rumors that his father, Mr. Robert Pierre, gave him away to a vodou priest named Thibodeaux in exchange for getting rich.

Thibodeaux was the most powerful vodou priest in the area. Most people knew that once Robert met Thibodaux, he became very rich, and every year, he had to offer sacrifices to the demons, including burnt offerings of goats, cows, pigs, and chickens. He took them by surprise because they thought that only animals were the extent of his sacrifices until one day, Thibodeaux asked him about the human sacrifice of a family member and was thus too late because their fate was sealed.

In the month of December, Robert went to see Thibodaux. Thibodeaux told him, "Don't forget you signed a contract with me to give me a male chick every year for three years. It was meant that you were going to give me a male child from your first to your third boy child, and I am going to take the first this year."

Right away, Robert knew what Thibodaux was talking about. "What do you mean you are going to take him this year?" Robert almost yelled at Thibodaux.

"Yes, I am taking your first son. When we made your promissory note, you agreed that you were going to give a chick once a year for three years. That's exactly what I meant. I don't care if you have many wives. I will take a boy from each one, but you have to make sure that you have a child ready each year for the next three years, or I will take you and your wife."

"I did not sign any note," replied Robert.

"We don't deal with paper here. Your verbal promise is all we accept."

Robert got upset. However, he had to sacrifice a child to Thibodeaux in order for him to keep the wealth that the demons had given to him.

Robert was naïve though. At first when he signed the contract because it says a chick, not a child. He thought that every year, he was going to bring a real chicken. He did not know that he sold his first three sons to the vodou priest to get rich.

The next day, he brought the chicken to Thibodaux; within a month, his second son, Kerry, passed away, Kerry was seven years old.

Kerry had a fever. The fever wasn't too bad. The mother sent Kerry to school. Once he arrived, a man came to the school, requesting that the teacher release Kerry to him. The teacher said that he could not release Kerry to a complete stranger; he did not know the man.

At once, Kerry began to vomit blood in the school. The teachers and the principal panicked. The man left but told the teacher to tell Kerry's mother and father that the person who was the messenger said, "Thibodeaux was going to take the child's life soon."

Everyone in the area knew the power of vodou. They knew who Thibodaux was. Thibodaux advertised his business of making people get rich. He was one of the most powerful vodou priests in the area. The teacher sent a messenger to the Pierres with the news. Robert wasn't home, but Liana was there.

At once, Liana called her father and mother to explain the situation while Kerry's fever got worse. When Kerry arrived at home, he told his dad, "Dad, I see blood."

Robert said, "Where?"

He said, "In my mouth."

The grandpa went to a vodou priest named Ozanfè. The father, Mr. Pierre, went to Thibodeaux. When the grandpa arrived at Ozanfè's, Ozanfè told him, "I can't do anything for you. The father of the child has a contract with Thibodeaux for human sacrifice every year for three years." And Ozanfè said to the grandpa, "Your grandson already died. I can show him to you right now."

Ozanfè pulled a mirror, and then the grandpa saw his grandson appear. "Is that him?" Ozanfè asked.

"Yes, that's him," the grandpa answered.

"He is gone," said Ozanfè.

When Mr. Robert arrived, Thibodeaux said, "You knew what you agreed to. I can't do anything for you, and you have to have another son or I will take your father, your wife, and mother. I do not want your daughter. She is not in the contract."

Three days later, Kerry died.

The entire area of Zorangé, Bar-de-La Croix, Coraille, and Tibras learned the story that Robert gave his sons to vodou in order to get rich. After the child died, the funeral was completed.

The next day, they went to visit the cemetery, but the tomb was empty. Robert and Liana had no boys, only their daughter, but he also had to combine three large spaces to create a bedroom in order to put a tiny snake there that was given to him by Thibodeaux. He wouldn't have any control of the snake even after he made his third human sacrifice. Thibodeaux, later on, asked Robert to sacrifice his mother or father, or he was going to lose his wife because it was a requirement on his agreement to give an adult male chicken or two adult females chicken.

Robert's life became so miserable. He did not know what to do. His hope then was on his daughter, Bethany, he had with his first wife. He lost two sons with her, but the daughter did not die because Thibodaux did not want a girl. His father, on the other hand, knew the story. He went to Ozanfè again; one of the most powerful and popular voodoo priests in Haiti to secure his life and that of his wife. As soon as he arrived, Ozanfè told him, "I see you coming to protect yourself and your wife?"

He said, "Yes."

"You need to act fast or you, or your wife will die," said Ozanfè.

The grandpa, who is Robert's father, said to Ozanfè, "Yes, this is the only reason I am here. I would like to act fast."

Ozanfè sent Robert's father back and asked him to come back the next day with his wife and a rooster.

Mr. Al went back the next day with the rooster. Ozanfè told him that his son, Robert would die because there was no other way he could spare his life, or he would be in trouble with Ozanfè. He washed them with dirty and smelly water and sent them back home.

Ozanfè told Mr. Al that when Robert dies, he must put the snake and all his money in the coffin and send him away with a vodou spell to spare the rest of the family.

Three days later, Mr. Al did exactly that. Robert died, but Liana was going to die at once as well. She had to convert into Protestantism right away with her daughter. She had to leave the house and never touch anything belonging to Robert, or she would never save a child, even if she herself would survive.

TALE 7

MASTER OF MOREAU AND UNCLE HISMERA

M R. FILS, UNCLE Hismera's father, told him in early 1970 that if he does not feed the dead, he will encounter one misfortune after the next. It was right after Duvalier demanded the Tontons Macoutes to arrest every man they could put their hands on and to go to applaud Duvalier during his January 1 Independence Day speech. Mr. Fils was one of the men who got arrested. It was when he got back that he spoke to Fils, "The dead have done a lot for us. You must feed them every year, especially Master Moreau. Master Moreau is an immortal god who followed us from Africa. He has been our protector. We never want him to get angry and go back to Africa. When I die, every year on October 1, you must kill cows, sheep, goats, pigs, and chickens. Always prepare food and take it to the forest of Moreau to Master Moreau, and he will eat and be satisfied. But the most important thing is not to forget that Master Moreau loves blood. If he does not find animal blood to drink, he will come to your house and suck the blood of your children. What you need to do is after you sacrifice the animals, put the blood in separate bowls according to the kind of animal, then put it on top of the sycamore tree in the middle of the forest, then he will come to drink it before he eats the flesh of the animals.

"Master Moreau is satisfied with whatever you give him. Don't just give Master Moreau meat. He eats plantains, yams, sweet potatoes, and breadfruits. And it is only once a year you have to feed him.

"You don't have to do anything. Just put the food on top of the large fig tree or the sycamore tree, and Master Moreau will come to get it. If you put the food after October 1, you will hear from Master Moreau that he is hungry. Hopefully, he will not enter the house and begin to drink blood from the children."

There was a large tree where the food was supposed to be exposed for Master Moreau. Fils told Hismera that it would be very dangerous if he did not prepare the food for Master Moreau. He could put himself and his family in danger. Hismera had never seen Master Moreau. He did not know how Master Moreau looked like.

Hismera said to his wife, "Those old folks have something to say. They want us to do vague things, but I will not be stupid to perform barbarian acts, not even for my father."

"I can't believe you said that about Fils," his wife, Annie, said to him. "Your father is a man that is privy to his own thoughts. If he did not know, he would not have said it. You should listen to him."

"I am not going to follow his vodou principles. Once he dies, his vodou spirit would leave with him," answered Hismera.

"I think you don't know what you are talking about," Annie said. "Vodou never leaves your family. It follows one from generation to the next generation unless one gives his life to Christ."

"Okay. We are not going to argue about it, Annie. But I need to tell you now that I will not give my life to your Christ. And I plan not to give food to Master Moreau."

"Thank you. I got enough," said Annie.

Hismera wanted to continue with the conversation. "You seem to believe in Satan while you believe in Jesus, huh, Annie?" Hismera asked.

"I do not put my faith in Satan, but I know he exists. Jesus himself had trouble with his in the wilderness if you read Matthew, chapter 4. He is a liar. I can also believe that Master Moreau can exist because if your generation has been following an evil spirit, that evil spirit will follow their children if they do not accept the blood of Christ. So I do not want you to feed Master Moreau, but I want you to come to Christ, or Master Moreau will take over you," said Annie.

"We will see," answered Hismera.

Annie did not answer again.

September 31 arrived; Hismera did not prepare any food for Master Moreau, but he was kind of afraid that something would happen to him. "If nothing happened," he said to himself, "I would know that my father was stupid for killing all those animals to throw away in the forest for so many years, and this practice had been going on for many, many generations."

On October 2, Hismera got up. He woke up one of his sons by the name of Nosteur for him to go and feed the animals with him. Upon arrival at the field, Nosteur said to Hismera, "Daddy, I see blood."

"Where do you see the blood?" Hismera asked Nosteur.

"Right here, Daddy. I saw the blood right after we left the house, but I did not want to tell you anything. But the trail of blood continues."

Then Hismera saw the blood. He panicked. He looked up and began to walk in the field; he found seven of his cows on the ground. He did not see any sign on the animals that could tell him what happened to them. He turned one of the cows over, and he saw marks from a hold in the cow's neck. Right away, he did not call the police because he knew what was wrong. He grabbed his son, and they ran home.

When they almost arrived home, his three-year-old son, Mark, came to meet with him.

"Daddy," he said, "I see blood all over the house. He ate Benita."

Hismera looked and saw a trail of blood going from his house to the forest. Hismera ran to the forest and followed the blood. When he arrived there, he saw a huge cave. His wife was sitting by the cave, lamenting.

"What happened?" Hismera asked his wife.

"Your lunatic vampire ate Benita."

He began to prepare the food at once. There were people sitting in the courtyard, and they saw a huge white blanket coming toward them, calling, "Hismera, Hismera, and Hismera."

Then Master Moreau replied, "I am not a vampire. I am hungry. When Fils was alive, I never got hungry. You need to prepare food for me as your father told you, or you will not be able to live in my habitation."

"You could ask. You did not have to kill my daughter," replied Hismera. "I killed her because you believed that I am nonexistent. Now you know that I am here to serve you as long as you respect me. If you do not respect me, I will destroy you."

Hismera sent for the area chief to come to help him with the situation. While Hismera was sitting at his balcony with his wife, the area chief and some visitors were thinking they could prepare to kill Master Moreau; it looked to him as if he was in a dream. Master Moreau appeared in front of his door.

"Hismera! Hismera! Where are you?"

Everybody ran away. Hismera came out. He saw something that looked like a black blanket, but its head was a snake.

Hismera said, "Where are you going, Master Moreau? What do you want from me?"

The blanket answered, "Don't you dare talk to me like this, or I can make your life miserable. Your father, your great-grandfathers never created any problems for me. Tomorrow is October 3. When Fils was still living I found my food and my water on October 1. I never asked for more. If you want me to create trouble for you, I can. I am capable of destroying everything you own, including killing you and your family. The only reason I have not done so is because of your father, Fils. He was good to me. I am ready for the food by midnight tonight. If you don't bring it, then you would know who Master Moreau is."

Then the blanket took off. It walked slowly until he arrived at the forest, and Hismera was looking at it in awe. With its wind, it blew a few banana trees away. All the chickens and other animals were howling. They had never seen anything as startling as that before.

The area chief ran. He did not say a word to Hismera.

"Where are you, Chief?" Hismera called. "Oh, you Tontons Macoutes are here to steal and kill and take money from people. Look, when I have a big problem, I called you, and you ran! I hope you all go to hell."

Annie replied, "Hismera, I told you, in Haiti, there is no hope besides God. You count on Erzilie. She fails you. You count on the police, and they fail you. Why don't you try Jesus?"

"I will someday, darling, but not now," Hismera replied.

On that day, Hismera called everyone in the area to help him with the preparation of the food. About two dozen men took the food to the forest to Master Moreau. Two days later, Master Moreau walked back to Hismera's house. He began to call, "Hismera, Hismera, and Hismera."

Everyone who saw the blanket ran away. Its wind could throw one away.

Hismera stayed at a distance and said, "What is going on now? I brought you the food."

"Yes," Master Moreau answered, "I found the food. I ate, and my stomach is full. I come to thank you, but I hope this never happens again."

Hismera bowed to the blanket and said "No, Master. It won't happen no more." Then Hismera watched Master Moreau leave his house.

Hismera had to bring the food to Master Moreau every year for many years until there was a time that he had no animals anymore to offer. He began to ask the neighbors for help. That year, every neighbor said that they could not afford it. There was a shortage of food in the area of Moreau, and people did not have money. Then his wife suggested that he convert to Protestantism.

The pastor came and prayed for the wife. Hismera was afraid to convert. The pastor told him, "Once you become a Christian, the blood of Christ will protect you and your family. You would never see any sign of this blanket again."

He accepted to join the Protestant Church, and ever since, the blanket never appeared again. Hismera and his family were then freed from the passing of these demonic spirits to the new generations.

The last time I saw Hismera and his family, they were singing this beautiful song, "I will not give glory to Satan, and Jesus alone deserves the glory. I am singing, singing glory to the Lord. I am singing the love that Jesus has for me. Praise, praise the Lord. I am singing the love that Jesus has for me."

TALE 8

KARANDELI, THE MYSTERY COW, AND THE FACELESS OLD MAN

THE COW REMAINED a mystery to everyone in Bainet since it appeared in February of 1970 to this day, but it became a reality when it killed Vyekò and his zombies on that summer day.

It happened suddenly. We heard a voice singing, but no one could see the person singing, "Karandeli, Karandeli, Karandeli, Karandeli." And there was a drumbeat afterward.

Those who claim to see the back of the man dressed in black, claimed that when they called him, "Hey! Who are you?" he turned and there is no face. The cow brought complete chaos into our lives because it produced fear in our minds from one generation to the next.

Most people thought the cow belonged to someone at Polycarpe while others thought the cow belonged to Jose in Lafeyard, to Hilary at Gory, to Jacob in Lunette, or Rubien in Gandou until Ozanfè revealed that the cow had been around Grand Ravine for two decades or more, and the cow is the spirit of Father Tame, grandfather of Vyekò. And the faceless man is a spirit that he brought with him as a slave from Africa.

The spirit happened to be a great drummer. Vyekò was a great drummer because the spirit had thought him how to play the drum. There was a time in December when everyone heard the drum and the singing. People awaken from sleep to dance as the drum beat and the song continued, "Karandeli, Karandeli, Karandeli, Karandeli."

The cow was a protection for the fifth section of the commune of Bainet. There is a faceless man who associates with the cow and he lives in the forest at Grande Ravine. Sometimes you see the cow, and other times it is the faceless old man who walks with his drum. Sometimes kids try to follow the drum beat and the song to the forest, and most of the time, they do not return.

The faceless man doesn't kill children, but he takes their *ti bon ange* (little soul) to serve him, and he creates a choir with them. There are testimonies of those who heard the children sing behind the faceless man as he sings aloud.

Thieves barely existed in the area because the faceless old man, who had the power to turn into a cow, killed every thief on the first strike. But he did not only kill thieves. When strangers come to the forest, he asked them to tell him where they are going and why they are there. He is invisible when he is asking those questions, and he won't let anyone leave unless one answers. If they are there for a good cause, he beats the drum and sings for them, "Karandeli, Karandeli, Karandeli, Karandeli." They would follow the drum as they danced to the perfect drumbeat.

The story began like this. A man named Vyekò, who was a great landowner, decided to get rich. He went to a popular vodou priest named Ozanfè to help him capture zombies to work in his fields and to help him catch thieves.

Ozanfè was a young man then at the age of nineteen, practicing magic under the direction of his father and grandfather, who were still alive, but he was already popular throughout Haiti. Nobody would realize how young he was because of his long beard. Behind his house, there is a great forest called the Grande Ravine.

When he arrived at Ozanfè's home, Ozanfè asked him, "What are you here for?"

Vyekò bowed his head before Ozanfè, who sat in a rocking chair in his long robe of many colors. His beard almost reached the floor, and he had multiple gold chains on his neck and large bracelets on both his wrists. Above him were two human heads, just cut. The legs were cut and placed in big bowls on each side of his chair.

"Father, I am here to see how you can help me to get rich."

Mr. Vyekò's eyes went straight in the bowls. His heart was beating too fast.

Ozanfè raised his head, "What's your name?"

"My name is Vyekò," he answered.

At once, a parrot began to call him by name in another room. "Vyekò, Vyekò. Welcome to Ozanfè's home, Vyekò."

Vyekò turned to look for the voice that was calling him. Then the curtain where the voice was heard inside the room was shoved aside. But no one came out. He raised his head and looked at the two heads dripping blood. He felt within himself that he must run.

"I have no problem turning you into a rich man right now, but there are prices to pay," Ozanfè answered. Ozanfè continued, "But before we continue, tell me a little bit about yourself. Where are you from? Who referred you to me?"

Before Vyekò answered Ozanfè, he recalled the curtain that was shoved aside, and he did not see any hands. He looked toward the door. He looked above his head to check the two heads that were leaking blood and the legs cut in the two bowls. He was curious; trying to see what was going on in that dark room. A faceless man appeared at the door. He panicked.

"Oh, shit!" he said it so loudly. Then he looked at Ozanfè. "I am sorry, Papa Ozanfè. I am sorry!"

Ozanfè sat there unmoved. "You are not going to answer me?" Ozanfè shouted.

"Oh, yes!" Vyekò answered. "I am from the premises of Polycarpe, Bainet. I am the son of Octave, the grandson of Tame of Polycarpe."

"Ah," Ozanfè answered. "Oh, I know your family very well. The revolutionist! I remember my grandfather sent a regiment of bizango to get Tame. He fought them all. He won too. They are powerful too."

"I did not know that," responded Vyekò.

"You wouldn't know. Those guys keep everything secret.

"Why are you coming to me for help while your parents have more power than anyone else in Bainet and even more than I am? In fact, he is the most powerful man on the whole island. Do you know your grandfather Tame? Tame was so powerful, and no man could conquer him even in his death. He fought like hell."

"I did not know that, Father Ozanfè, until you told me now."

Vyekò turned his head toward that dark room again. Then he heard a woman begin to sing. She sang beautifully, "Karandeli, Karandeli, Karandeli, Karandeli." She had the voice of Carole Demesmin, one of the best Haitian singers.

He backed away from Ozanfè. Ozanfè laughed. "Are you trying to run? And why are you afraid of me when I just told you that you come from one of the most powerful families on the island? Go ahead and run! Are you telling me I am a demon?" Ozanfè told Vyekò.

"Oh no, Father, I would never say something like that."

"Why not? I eat human flesh sometimes. I am not going to eat you, but I eat those who think they can challenge me." He looked behind him. He looked right then left, and then he raised his head to take a quick glance at those heads above his head. "I don't think you will be able to do business with me. You are not a brave man at all," said Ozanfè.

"I am sorry, Father Ozanfè."

"Oh, you're still here. I thought you left." There was a silence. Then Ozanfè said to Vyekò, "If a man decides to come to my house, he must be brave."

"I know that, Father!" Vyekò responded while he was shaking. "Who told you about my family? How do you know they were powerful?" Vyekò placed his hands on his mouth, and then he said, "That's scary."

"What's scary?" Ozanfè replied.

"Everything you just told me," replied Vyekò.

At once, Vyekò heard a band singing and an accordion was playing. He turned his eyes to look.

"Don't worry about this. My zombies, they are enjoying themselves," said Ozanfè. Then a large black dog appeared out of nowhere and sat next to Vyekò.

Vyekò turned slowly and looked at the dog. In his mind, he said, "What a frightening dog."

The dog sat there until Ozanfè said to the dog, "Come and sit next to me!"

The dog moved and sat on a chair next to Ozanfè. Then the dog turned to a beautiful woman, who began to sing the same song she was singing before. The song goes, "Mwen pat jam konnen mizè. Mwen pat jam konnen traka avan manman, papa m mwen te mouri. A dix ans manm kite m, a douz ans Papa sevre m, yo lagay ap viv sou tè. Denis, Denise O Bondye, plike w rele m rele m kote map kite yo?" (I never knew misery. I never knew trouble before Mom and Dad died. At ten years old, my mother left me. At twelve, my father gave up on me. Denis, Denise, my fraternal twins. Oh God, since you call me, where am I going to leave them?)

Ozanfè said to Vyekò, "Don't tell me that your father did not transfer his power to you before he died?"

"No, Father," Vyekò replied. "My father died in a car accident. He died very young." At once, Vyekò felt tired. He closed his eyes.

"Are you sleeping while I am talking to you?" Ozanfè asked him.

Vyekò opened his eyes, he did not see Ozanfè. He saw a tall, dark-skinned man with large eyes and wide eyebrows sitting on the chair where Ozanfè was sitting. When he looked closely, he realized it was his father who died long ago, sitting on the chair. Vyekò got up.

The father said, "Ha-ha! Why are you here?"

Vyekò turned. He was surrounded by zombies.

Then he heard Ozanfè said, "You are aware that your dad died long ago! I have been having him here." Vyekò looked up; he saw Ozanfè standing on a pedestal. Vyekò began to shake. "Why are you here?" Ozanfè asked.

Before Vyekò answered, Ozanfè walked toward Vyekò in his long robe of many colors on. His long beard almost touched the earth. Vyekò felt that he had to scream, but tears filled his eyes. He sweated. While Vyekò was looking at Ozanfè, both his dad and the woman disappeared. Ozanfè raised his chin. "Tell me what you are scared of. Do you think I might ask you to give me the secret? It is true. I need to know how to undo the power that your parents have."

Vyekò raised his head. "Father Ozanfè, I don't know any secrets. If I had any secrets, why do I come to you?"

Ozanfè said, "You do not have to tell me. I have your *ti bon ange* (little soul) here already."

JOSEPH P. POLICAPE

Vyekò looked. He saw himself standing on the opposite side. His clone was bleeding. "Oh God, do not let me die here!" Vyekò cried.

"Where did you see God?" Ozanfè replied. Then Ozanfè bore at Vyekò with bad eyes and walked back to his seat. Ozanfè said, "If you knew I was going to take your soul in my kingdom, you would enter Protestantism. I know the Protestants are very powerful. They give me lots of trouble here. Nobody can fight those people, but if you do not convert, it is too late. You are in my kingdom right now. I don't know yet if I will grant you mercy."

Vyekò raised his head. On his right-hand side, the head was still hanging from the ceiling, and the two hands that were in the two bowls on the left-hand side were still there. He looked behind him; he saw a basket filled with meat. The head was still spurting blood. The guy's eyes were still open. His beard was still on his face. Ozanfè said, "I just killed this one for supper tonight."

In his mind, Vyekò thought, *What on earth am I doing here? This might be my last day on this earth. Is he going to kill me for meat, or is he going to take my zombie to work for him?*

Ozanfè said, "Calm down! I need you as a friend. I'll help you, but you have to help me as well." Ozanfè called one of his zombies, "Tipay! Come here!"

Vyekò saw a beautiful woman came out. She was dressed beautifully as if she is going to a party.

"Show this man how we dance here!" She held both of her hips and turned from side to side, then back and forth. Ozanfè laughed then he said, "Go show him where to take a shower and prepare a meal for him. He is my friend."

Ozanfè came forward and gave Vyekò a hug and said, "I feel bad when you arrived here. If I knew the type of family you came from, I would have never taken your father and your grandfather. They both are here. Your grandfather, oh! Tame, he is a rebel in spite that he is very old. He has been with us for forty years because my father took his zombie when he was in his late thirties. He is immortal. He has a power that was given to him by his father. He transferred the gift to your father. I am not sure if they had given you the gift and shared the secret with you. I thought you had it, but it seems your father did not get a chance to transfer it to you. If he did, I would have been on my knees right now. Go take a shower and eat. We will talk later."

While in the shower, Vyekò recalled his father said once to him, "I am a mighty man. I have lots of power, but I do not want you to engage in magic when you grow up. I am miserable. I can't sleep on my bed at night. Every night, I become all kinds of animals and go eat other animals in the forest. You should convert to become a Protestant."

Vyekò felt better then, but he asked himself, "Why didn't I convert to be a Protestant?"

He took his clothes off. He looked on his left side; he saw a room filled with zombies, but there was a beautiful zombie woman looking at him as if saying, "Wow, he is big!" She put her right hand in her mouth.

While the other zombies were busy, they worked on all kinds of projects inside Ozanfè's palace. Vyekò tried to cover his private parts with his hands, and then the zombie woman came forward and closed the bathroom door. After Vyekò finished taking his shower, Tipay came and walked him to the dining room table. She pulled a chair. He sat at the table, and Ozanfè arrived and sat with him. Inside his soup, he saw fingers in it. His heart started beating fast. He yelled, "Oh God, what's that?"

Ozanfè looked at him and laughed. "If you were not my friend, you would die spitefully. You don't say a thing when you come to my house, and I serve you. You eat without saying a word."

Vyekò ate. Then he bowed. "Thank you, Father Ozanfè!"

"You're welcome," Ozanfè replied. Ozanfè asked Vyekò, "Son, can you flash back? You never remember that your dad talked to you about his power or your grandpa? Don't lie to me!"

Vyekò was thinking. "Yes, Father. I remember when I was about eight years of age, my father told me, 'I am a mighty man. I have lots of power, but I do not want you to engage in magic when you grow up. I am miserable. I can't sleep on my bed at night. Every night, I become all kinds of animals, and I go eat other animals in the forest. You should convert into Protestantism before I die, but if you don't, I have to transfer my power to you before I die.'

"Another time, I was about ten years old. My father called and said, 'Vyekò, you are a man now. I have many things that I would not tell your mother, but I can tell you. In our family, we have lots of power. Eventually, I will transfer them to you. In our family, we do not die. When we die, before our funeral, we return to a forest to become wild animals. We never die. We can become any animal we wish. No power can conquer us. If we go to jail, we can return. This is a power that we brought with us from Africa. The only people that are more powerful than us are the true Christians. Ah, they are very powerful. When they mention the name of Jesus, no power can stand before them.'

"That was the only thing that father said to me. A week later, he died suddenly."

Ozanfè was silent for a moment, then he said, "I believe you. You would not have come here if you had their powers. That means the power is now lost because they cannot transfer it anymore."

Vyekò looked kind of disappointed. He asked, "If you have them, can you make them give you the secret?"

Ozanfè looked at Vyekò. "You are tired, my friend. I am going to stop torturing you. You need to go to bed." Ozanfè asked one of his female zombies to escort Vyekò to bed.

The woman straightened her hand and gestured to Vyekò to get into bed. Then she entered behind Vyekò and closed the door. Vyekò even became more fearful. Vyekò asked her, "Are you staying?"

"Yes," the zombie answered. "Papa Ozanfè sent me to sleep with you tonight." She began to unbutton Vyekò's pants.

"Do not do that!" Vyekò exclaimed to the woman.

"You do not have the power to tell me what to do or not to do," the woman replied to him.

They both lay in bed. Vyekò gave her his back. The zombie moved very close to Vyekò; Vyekò could feel her breath warm on his back. "Are you going to bite me?" Vyekò asked her.

"No," she answered through her nose. "I am here to entertain you." Then she began to slip her hand down his underwear.

"Ah . . .," Vyekò cried, "it feels good." Vyekò forgot that she was a zombie. He turned around and got on top of the zombie.

The zombie said, "Ah . . . you remind me of the time I was a living being with my husband."

Vyekò laid with the zombie, and he wanted to ask her a lot of questions about being a zombie, but he was too fearful that Ozanfè might have set him up.

In the morning, the zombie brought Vyekò back to Ozanfè.

"I never give my clients women to go to bed with anyone, but I consider you a friend. I wanted to make you feel comfortable," Ozanfè said to Vyekò. "How was it?" Ozanfè asked Vyekò.

"It was really good, but I did not know zombies could have sex."

"He is a superman," the woman replied.

Then Ozanfè said, "You heard her. They still have feelings, and some of them are not completely brain-dead like Tipay. They have real feelings although they would not know if they were to leave unless somebody undue them. You see all these bottles? Each one has his or her soul in one of them. One has to release the soul from the bottle, then have them eat salt for them to be able to survive as human again."

"How do you know which one is what bottle?"

"Each bottle is marked by something to identify each one, but unless you know, you won't be able to identify them." It seemed that Tipay was listening to the conversation, but rather, she was looking at Vyekò. Ozanfè laughed. "I think Tipay wants to keep you here."

"Don't say that please, Papa" Vyekò replied to Ozanfè.

Ozanfè looked at Vyekò. He looked very serious this time, and he said, "Do not bargain for your soul."

Vyekò smiled. "I will let you go home. Promise me you will take your evil grandfather with you, and you will not bring him back. Otherwise, I will keep you here." Vyekò nodded to say yes. "I do not want you to nod your head to me," shouted Ozanfè.

"I say yes, Father," replied Vyekò. There was silence. Then Vyekò raised his head. "When I take him, would I be able to manage him, Papa Ozanfè?"

"Yes. He wants to go back to his territory," replied Ozanfè.

All of a sudden, the drum began to beat. One could hear the song in the air, "Karandeli, Karandeli, Karandeli, Karandeli," but no singer was visible. Ozanfè got up and began to dance. All the zombies began to dance. Vyekò had to dance too.

"You see," said Ozanfè, "he is somewhere listening to our conversation. He wants to go home, but everybody is going to miss the drum beat and the singing."

"I gave your father away to a friend of mine last week. He is a powerful vodou priest in Jeremie. He took Tame to Jeremie with him. I hope to never see him or hear from him again, but knowing that he is a rebel, it is unlikely he won't return."

"If my father returns, I would love to have him," responded Vyekò. "I am glad you say that. We will see. He is very hard to handle, but who knows. He might do well with you."

"I will give you your grandfather to you before you leave. He turned into a cow. He turned into a faceless man whenever he wished, but he can no longer transfer the power to his family. Their spirits will be alive, but no man will have the power," said Ozanfè. "When you came here, he was the one who was singing and playing the drum. Sometimes, I hear a band in my house. I can see everything, but this band is so invisible. I am unable to see, and I do not know its destination. If I put him out, he enters the house any time he wants to. He can't harm me, but he keeps me under control. He only allows me to sleep when he wants to."

Ozanfè walked with Vyekò and went to a large field. He pointed his finger. "Do you see all those men working over there in the field? They are all zombies. I have seventy-five of them in the field right now, and I have others elsewhere. You can go there and show me which one you would like to have. Let's go! I can give you up to three and your father."

As soon as Vyekò arrived among the zombies, he did not see anyone. He looked at Ozanfè. Ozanfè looked at him, and he laughed. "You will not be able to see them because zombies do not let people see their faces. They hide when they see you. They can also change their faces if they do not want you to see them. When you have zombies, never let them eat salt. They all will escape because their consciousness will return to them unless you take away their soul completely."

"How do you take their soul completely?" Vyekò asked.

"Do you think I will give you the secret? Of course not!" he replied. "But remember I showed you the bottles where I kept each one of them," Ozanfè stated. "Everybody stand up!" Ozanfè yelled.

At once, Vyekò saw all the zombies stood up. "If you know any of them, do not identify them. Never go anywhere to say that you went to Ozanfè, and then you saw zombies. I will know you do that, and you will die if you do that."

"I would never do that, Father Ozanfè," replied Vyekò. Vyekò pointed to five zombies that he would like to take. He took two women and three men.

"Is that all you want?" Ozanfè asked Vyekò.

Vyekò laughed. "How am I going to feed them? I am not rich like you."

"Well, after you leave this place, you are going to be rich," replied Ozanfè. Then Ozanfè walked with him in a forest. He sang the song, "Karandeli, Karandeli, Karandeli, Karandeli, Karandeli, Karandeli."

A big cow appeared out of nowhere under the sycamore tree. And Ozanfè said, "You can take this one with you. This is your grandfather. He is immortal and tough to handle. He wants to go back to his premises. There is a large forest behind your house. Release him there. Never cut the forest, or he would create lots of trouble for you. He will run everywhere and nonstop. The only way we can get rid of him is to send him back to Africa. I do not have the secret of sending him back there."

"How do you know I have a forest at the back of my house, Papa Ozanfè?"

"I know everything. Go! Take your zombies with you. Take the cow! Do what I tell you to do. Drink this before you go, or your zombies will stay here with me. And if you let your zombies stay here, not even the Protestants will be able to get your zombies back because I will fry them."

Ozanfè handed a glass of red stuff; it looked like blood to Vyekò to drink.

"I will see you within a year."

Vyekò left that day. When he went outside, the rain was falling to earth very strongly. There was darkness outside, but the sky was still blue, the moon was not pregnant, or he would have been able to see his way better. He tried to hold on to his zombies to make sure they did not escape. The road was heavy with mud. Vyekò had to walk ahead with the cow, and the zombies were behind him. He was scared. He kept looking back to make sure that the zombies stayed with him, and they were not trying to kill him.

"Don't look back. When I need you, I will call you."

Vyekò took the zombies and his cow, and he left Ozanfè's house. The zombies walked ahead of him, they never looked up. Whatever he told them, they did it. They never said no. The cow never disobeyed either. The cow followed him until he arrived at Daraspin.

He brought the cow to the Grand Ravine Forest. Grand Ravine was the most beautiful forest in the commune of Bainet.

A few days after, Vyekò released the cow in the forest. The cow went down to the river to drink. The neighbors reported that they saw a huge cow coming down to drink. The cow seemed to have a chain on its neck because they heard the chain when the animal was walking down the river and the sound of the drum as well as the song, "Karandeli, Karandeli, Karandeli, Karandeli, Karandeli, Karandeli."

Some of the neighbors would not come out but would get up and dance. From then on, whenever the animal came down, people knew it, not only because people heard the noise, but they also saw the large hoof prints that the animal left on the ground, and the pond was almost dry after the animal drank there.

For some of the neighbors, the cow was the god of fertility. First, every time the animal came down to drink, it rained the next day. Also, the animal came down twice a year during the planting seasons. There was another mystery about the cow when the animal came down. It begged. People also reported that they saw a faceless man near the forest. People thought the faceless man lived in the forest. People saw him walking. His hair was never combed. He wore blue jeans. He wore a black T-shirt but had no face.

The faceless man never talked to anyone. He never allowed people to get close to him; he disappeared. Some people who have fields near the area said that sometimes they put food on the coal and left it for a little while; the man came and turned the food from one side to another, and sometimes got the food ready for them, but he would never eat the food.

The faceless old man left a note to Vyekò one day and said, "Do not be afraid. I am your grandfather. I did not cooperate with Ozanfè because I did not want him to have control over me. Promise me, you will never tell him. I will give you the secret. Ozanfè thought we will never be able to transfer it. He is wrong. I am in communication with Octave. He already destroyed the house of that vodou priest in Jeremie, and he is on his way to us. And he will never be able to conquer your soul as he did me and your father. I can't show you my face, but I will protect your field and the forest. The only time I will create trouble for you is if you touch my forest. It is my home."

Before the cow was released to the forest, thieves used to steal cows, horses, goats, and pigs in that area. But since the cow came into the commune, a strange thing happened; every time a thief took something, we woke up and found the thief dead. And if a thief took an animal, the animal would be tied next to him, or if he stole food, the thing he stole would be next to him at the marketplace.

Two days after he received the note, Vyekò's wife was cooking. She left the food on the coal and went inside the house and lay down. She fell asleep. When she woke up, the faceless old man came; he stirred the food, put it on low. He then watched all the dishes and the pots and brought some more wood to her. He left a note: "I am your neighbor. I live in the forest. Your food was getting burned. I helped you. I am also the one who watched the dishes. Do not be afraid. Everything is under control."

Once Vyekò heard the story from his wife, he consulted a vodou priest by the name of Darius. As soon as he arrived at the vodou priest's home, Darius said to him, "I know why you are here. Your grandfather's creation is making you terrified. You are dealing with a very powerful spirit. He is acting in your favor right now, but eventually, he will turn against you, as well as Ozanfè. You have a lot to deal with. If I were you, I would convert to Protestantism without talking to anyone.

"You will not be able to conquer either one of those two powers by flesh and blood. You need a stronger spirit, and that spirit is the spirit of God of heaven."

The vodou priest made a prediction. "You should never cut the forest. The day you cut it, the cow will destroy everything you have. You can't take it back to Ozanfè. Ozanfè will kill you before you get to his house, and the cow would not go either. This faceless man that comes to your house is the same cow," the vodou priest said. "Have you heard the story of your grandfather, Tame?" he asked Vyekò.

"Not really," Vyekò replied.

"Ah! There was a problem in Port Au Prince in the early 1800s. Jacmel and Cayes decided that they would not be part of Port-au-Prince anymore. They wanted to take independence from Port-au-Prince, but they could not do it unless they were able to control the entire *arrondissement*. Bainet refused to join. Jacmel decided to invade Bainet, but Tame was the mastermind behind the revolution. When Jacmel went to Bainet, they went to arrest Tame. Bainet had no weapon to fight Jacmel but fought Jacmel with their vodou power.

"When fifty policemen from Jacmel went to Tame's home, he told them, 'Come in!' They pulled their guns, trying to arrest him. When they tried to tie him, he invoked some spirit from Africa, and then he was able to disappear. Tame started stoning them. When he killed five of them, the rest ran away, and Bainet won the war. They offer a sacrifice to that spirit, and it remains with them ever since. The spirit is only connected to you if you are a family member. If you convert, it will have no choice but to go back to Africa because Jesus's blood will cover you.

"Ozanfè the father took your grandfather. When he was not satisfied, he took your father. He was so happy to give you back the grandfather. The son gave him back to you because if he continued to keep him, he was going to kill Ozanfè. If you had told him that you did not want to take the cow, he would not have given you those zombies, and he would have killed you."

Vyekò sat there, and he did not know what to do or what to answer. He asked Darius, "What can I do now?"

Darius responded, "Well, let me finish telling you the story. After your grandfather, Tame, died, Ozanfè was able to take his zombie. I do not know how he told his children before his death that when he died he was not going under the ground. Right after his funeral, they were ready to bury him. He became a cat and escaped. Ozanfè was angry, and he caused your father Octave to die in a car accident, and he took his zombie. He could not control him either. He killed most of Ozanfè's zombies before Ozanfè gave him back to a vodou priest in Jeremie. We don't know what he's doing in Jeremie right now. There is nothing you can do. You should convert to become a Protestant because Jesus is very powerful. He took away many souls from us."

Vyekò responded, "If I accept Jesus, what am I going to do with the zombies?"

"You got to release them, and you have to testify about all of this, then you will be freed from all evil spirits."

Vyekò responded, "I will think about it."

A few months after Vyekò went to see Darius, he looked at the forest. The forest was beautiful, and the wood became very expensive. While he was in bed with his wife, he said, "Darling, I am going to destroy the forest at Grande Ravine. Too much land is wasted."

His wife's name was Eunice. Eunice said, "You are crazy. What would you do with the prediction that says you can't destroy the forest? What about the faceless old man that told you if you destroy the forest, you are going to be in trouble? What is wrong with you? Please, Vyekò, leave the forest alone."

Vyekò was silent for a minute, then he said, "I promise you I will destroy the forest, and nothing will happen to me."

Eunice said, "If something happens to you, you are not going to know. You are going to die and leave me in trouble with the children."

Vyekò did not listen to his wife. He made up his mind to destroy the forest. Early in the morning, Vyekò was about to leave his house to go to the field. He saw a faceless old man arrived. His hair was never combed. He wore blue jeans and a black T-shirt. He said to Vyekò, "Last night, you told your wife that you are going to destroy the forest. Whenever you wish, you can destroy it, but remember, if you destroy the forest, you will have to find me another home. If you don't have another home for me and destroy the forest, I will destroy you and your family."

Vyekò was so afraid. The voice was loud, clear, and scary. The old faceless man disappeared then there was a big wind that threw Vyekò away and took down the roof of his house.

Vyekò went and destroyed the forest.

A month after he destroyed the forest, nothing happened to him. He said to his wife, "You see how much money we were going to lose if I listened to you? The dead have no power over the living. Thanks to Papa Ogoun, I am not crazy like you."

The wife answered, "Satan never forgets you unless you accept Jesus Christ as your personal savior. I have asked you to take the children to go to church and accept Jesus. You refused. Whenever your ancestors catch up with you, they will not be able to touch me or the children because I do not belong to them. I belong to God."

The next day, Vyekò woke up early. He went to the field. He put his zombies to work. He sat there supervising them at work. At once, he heard horses galloping; he saw the chickens flying, the goats and pigs were squealing. Vyekò moved farther to see what was going on. He thought it was a wild cat that was trying to eat the chicken because that was very common in Bainet. He saw a wild cow running all over the field. He looked farther; three of his zombies lay on the ground. He looked farther. Four of his cows, three of his horses, and two of his mules were lying on the ground dead. He recalled the prediction that the priest made to him a few months ago. He learned from his parents that evil spirits hate the cross. He crossed his hands in front of the cow. The cow took him with its horns and killed Vyekò.

During Vyekò's funeral the next day, Eunice, along with her two children, Jean-Paul and Murielle, wholeheartedly embraced her new faith and the salvation and blood of Christ.

That year, Karandeli took over the commune. The cow killed two dozen people in that one month. The drum was playing all day, all night, but it was different, and the singer was singing as if someone was crying, "Karandeli, Karandeli, Karandeli, Karandeli, Karandeli, Karandeli." But that time, each time the voice sang, it paused for a few seconds before the next "Karandeli" came out. The cow and the faceless man were sad because they had no other family members to hang on to. Eunice and her children were covered by the blood of Jesus; they could not pass near them.

One day, Eunice was about to go to bed, but she left the house where she and her husband used to live. Before she went to bed, she prayed with the children. When they went to bed, Jean-Paul had a dream. In the dream, he saw Karandeli running around the commune, killing people. He had a cross in his hand. He raised the cross toward Karandeli and said, "Karandeli, in the name of Jesus, I bind your power from you."

In the morning, Jean-Paul woke up and told his mother about the dream. He was eight years old at the time.

Nobody wanted to walk alone. They could hear the voice sing the song and heard the cow running, but not able to see it. That was the scariest part.

Many people went to the river together. There were about one hundred people at the river. Karandeli was coming. It ran faster than a car. The cow became invisible, so no one could see it. Jean-Paul was the only one who could see the cow. After the dream, he thought it might have been God who spoke to him that he needed to make a cross to scare Karandeli if he saw it coming. When he woke up that morning, he made a cross. Wherever he went, he went with the cross. Jean-Paul said to the people, "Here is Karandeli!"

Everybody said, "Are you crazy? Where is Karandeli?"

Jean-Paul said, "Here it is!"

Nobody but he could see Karandeli. Karandeli began to run toward the people. The cow was ready to kill.

Jean-Paul took the cross and knelt down. Then he prayed, "Oh, God, I do not believe in any other power but yours. I pray in the name of Jesus Christ, the king of kings, the lord of lords, the Lion from the tribe of Judas, give me power over this cow today. In Jesus's name, I pray."

He yelled, "Karandeli, I see your face. Karandeli, spirit from Africa, go back where you came from. In the name of Jesus, I bind you forever!"

The cow looked at the cross in Jean-Paul's hand. The cow fell on the ground, and it was set on fire. Then the cow became visible. Everyone now could see the cow on fire. Then it disappeared. Jean-Paul became a hero in the commune of Bainet.

TALE 9

THE WITCH STEPMOTHER AND CHIFFON

THIS STORY WAS told to me by my mother and Aunt Justine at different times when they came to visit me in Port au Prince during the summer vacations of 1970 and 1971, but for the same reason, evil catches up with evil, as the old folks used to say.

Chiffon was a bony ten-year-old girl who lived at Cité Cadet in Port-au-Prince with her father, his wife, two other sisters, and a brother. It was very common in Haiti for fathers with better means to support their children, taking them to have their married wife to raise. Many of them ended up dying from malnutrition and abuse.

Chiffon's mother was a poor woman who had a tryst with the very wealthy Mr. Pourra, and from that quick love affair, Chiffon was born. In the household of her father and stepmother, she was mistreated. When the poor thing spoke, you could hear that the words were coming from her nose. One wondered how she walked on her skinny legs. She was responsible for cooking everything in the house, except she was not allowed to eat the food at the dining table like the rest of the family. She was an invisible human being.

Chiffon's mother, not knowing what her daughter was going through, was happy for she lived with her father, and she was able to go to school and eat well because the mother was very poor. her, not knowing what she was going through. Marie, her mother, was a good Christian, but due to misery, she fell in love with this well-to-do married man named Pourra.

Pourra married a woman named Pauline. She went by the name of Madame Pourra. Madame Pourra was a vodou worshiper and a witch.

She was a well-trained witch. She belonged to the society of witches called bizango, which made human sacrifices. They were carnivorous. Every year, this group had to make some type of human sacrifice. One member of the group had to offer a child from year to year as a sacrifice.

Madame Pourra was the stepmother of Chiffon, the beautiful, tall, bony ten-year-old girl. She mistreated Chiffon too. She abused the little girl verbally, mentally, and physically. "You will never be anything when you grow up. Come here, monster! Chiffon, did you hear? I said come here. This woman is a witch!"

"Here I am, madam!" Chiffon stood beside Madame Pourra.

"Where were you? Oh, this girl is a demon! I've never seen anything like this. I was calling her, and she was right there, yet she never answered."

"I answered, madam!"

"Oh, don't talk back to me, lady. She is a liar! I can't stand her. Do you think that you are going to cause my death so that you can eat my children alive in this house, Chiffon?" That was the way the stepmother used to talk and treat her stepdaughter. "Where are you, monster? You are the one I am calling, Chiffon, little monster!"

The stepmother used Chiffon as her slave, and she told the other children to treat the striking little girl as such. The word *chiffon* means rag, but her true name is Naomi. Mrs. Pourra changed Naomi's name to Chiffon when Mr. Pourra took custody of her and brought her to her evil stepmother.

Every morning, Chiffon had to wake up at 4:00 a.m. to prepare breakfast for her father, stepmother, and her half-brother and half-sisters. Every morning, around four thirty, Mrs. Pourra would call Chiffon, "Chiffon, where are you, little monster? Why this girl makes me talk so much. Are you done ironing the clothes?"

"Yes."

"Oh! Chiffon, how dare you answer me like that! You do not know how to say, 'Yes, madam'?"

"I am sorry, madam!"

"You'll be sorry, and tomorrow, you will do the same, monster!"

Mrs. Pourra never allowed Chiffon to call her mother. Chiffon must call her madam. She would have to iron their clothes, clean their shoes, and mop the floor. Then Chiffon had to take her older sister, Betty, to the bus stop, as well as the other children on two different trips. Betty was twelve years of age, and Chiffon was ten, but Chiffon got used to the abuse.

Mr. Pourra knew that Chiffon had been abused, but he never said anything to his wife or talk to Chiffon about what was going on because he loved his wife and children so much. Chiffon never told him anything either.

In fact, Chiffon was afraid of him. Chiffon, in her heart, blamed him for her abuse. "If my father loved me, he would have taken care of me or me with my mother who would treat me as a person," Chiffon used to say in her heart.

After Chiffon completed all the chores at the house, she would go to school at night—the little school at the back of the house. But that did not stop Chiffon from being a better reader and writer than Madame Pourra's children. It seemed that the misery helped Chiffon to grow steadily and strongly.

She learned how to live life. She knew every tactic in life. She woke up early and went to bed late. Chiffon almost never saw her biological mother; she was so poor, but Chiffon's mother was a woman of prayer. She prayed for her daughter daily, and at a very early age, she taught Chiffon how to pray.

One day, Madame Pourra came home, and there was no bread in the refrigerator. "Where are you, little monster? Oh! I can't see this little monster in my face anymore. She is useless. How come there is no bread in the house?"

"I am sorry, madam. You did not tell me to buy bread."

"Oh! Look at you. I don't know how many boyfriends this woman has. Go bring me two packs of bread right now! Don't stop to talk to your boyfriends on the street, and don't eat the bread. If you take a piece, I will see. I will stick a hot iron on your face. Do you hear me, little monster?"

Chiffon got frustrated at times, but she became such a strong child. Though she was only ten years old, she was the woman of the house. Mrs. Alexander, who lived across the street, always came closer to hear what Mrs. Pourra had been saying to the child.

One day, Mrs. Alexander said to Chiffon, "What kind of mother has to abandon you in the hands of this witch? You are ten years old, and you have been abused by this woman for a long time. Your father is not a man either. He carries the dress. What kind of father would see her daughter being mistreated like this and accept it?"

One day, Madame Pourra called Chiffon. "Little monster, where are you?" Chiffon came to her. "Make sure all the children's clothes are ready for the week. You will not have time to prepare them again because I am going to send you to some place for the week."

Chiffon did not say a word. She did whatever her stepmother asked her to do, but she prayed for God to guide her through life.

The time came for Madame Pourra to offer her sacrifice at the end of the year. She did not know what to do. She planned to give Chiffon to the regiment. At night, she said, "Chiffon, it is hot. I want you to sleep on the floor with all the children."

Mr. Pourra said, "Why do you want the children to sleep on the floor?"

"It is too hot, darling. They will sleep on the floor tonight."

She did not want to tell Chiffon alone to sleep on the floor because she did not want her husband to understand what was going on.

Madame Pourra helped Chiffon fix the bed this time on the floor as then most kids used to sleep on the floor. She put her two girls in the front and put Chiffon in the back, by the door. Her daughter, who was twelve, Chiffon dressed her and did whatever she wanted to do. She called for Chiffon to do it all for her. She learned from her mother that Chiffon was her slave.

Madame Pourra waited until the children slept. Then she began her magic prayer to put everyone in the house in deep sleep so that she can leave to meet with her regiment of demons. Then she unlocked the door.

Chiffon wasn't sleeping, but she pretended. In her mind, Chiffon was praying. Once Madame Pourra left, she knelt and recited Psalm 23 by heart. "The Lord is my shepherd. I have everything I need. He lets me rest in fields of green grass and leads me to quiet pools of freshwater. He gives me new strength. He guides me in the right paths, as he has promised. Even if I go through the deepest darkness, I will not be afraid, Lord, for you are with me. Your shepherd's rod and staff protect me. You prepare a banquet for me, where all my enemies can see me. You welcome me as an honored guest and fill my cup to the brim. I know that your goodness and love will be with me all my life, and your house will be my home as long as I live."

Chiffon waited after her stepmother unlocked the door and went to bed, then Chiffon took the nightgown from her sister Betty, and she put her own nightgown on Betty because her nightgown was completely different from Betty's. Chiffon's nightgown was a sackcloth. Then she changed places with Betty. She placed Betty in front of the door.

Around one o'clock in the morning, she heard noises. She moved farther from the door. The stepmother came, opened the door, pulled Betty out, killed her, and asked the regiment to help her carry the body. Mrs. Pourra danced all night. She laughed with the other witches. She was the first to be served the meat.

"I want the liver please." They brought her the liver. "Oh . . . well-done! It tastes very good."

One of the witches came to Mrs. Pourra and said, "You're lucky. You paid your debt now. I have to find one to give before January 1, or I am going to owe double."

Mrs. Pourra raised her dress very high so one can see her underwear. "I paid, my darling."

They went and had a great party. In the morning, she ran to her home. Time for her to go take care of the children. When she arrived at the house, her husband was still in deep sleep. She did her magic to awake him from sleep. Then she ran to the kitchen to prepare breakfast for the children, and her husband because she thought Chiffon was no more. She went into the kitchen. She clapped her hands. "Oh, what a beautiful night it was last night."

She thought that the father was not even going to notice if Chiffon was missing. She was going to say that Chiffon went to school and was kidnapped. She bumped into Chiffon in the kitchen. She began to yell and said, "I don't think Papa Ogoun would do this to me. I give Papa Ogoun food every year to watch over my children."

Chiffon answered, "I don't think my God would have done that to me either."

"What is going on?" Mr. Pourra exclaimed. "Oh! Oh! Where is my daughter?" Madame Pourra asked. "What daughter? What daughter are you talking about?"

Mr. Pourra ran to the kitchen. "What is going on?"

Madame Pourra could not say anything; it was like she was muted.

Mr. Pourra exclaimed again, "What daughter? Tell me what is going on."

Mrs. Pourra said, "Betty! Betty is what!" Mr. Pourra looked at Chiffon. "Chiffon, tell me what is going on!"

Chiffon told the father what she saw.

Mr. Pourra asked his wife, "Where is my daughter Betty?"

She answered, "They already killed her." Then Madame Pourra ran inside the bedroom. Mr. Pourra ran behind her. But he couldn't catch her because she had locked the bedroom door. Mr. Pourra called the police.

Once the police arrived, they broke a window, trying to enter the room; they saw Madame Pourra pull a gun and shoot herself. Her blood filled the room. Then Chiffon opened up and told her story, how long she had been abused and what Mrs. Pourra had done that night to give Chiffon to the regiment. She tricked Mrs. Pourra. Then Mrs. Pourra mistook her own daughter for Chiffon.

Mr. Pourra buried her and married Chiffon's mother, the poor woman named Marie. Chiffon grew up and became one of the most successful women in Port-au-Prince, and she and her remaining brothers and sister grew up together. The new Mrs. Pourra, the woman who used to be Marie, the poor woman who was the mother of Chiffon became the mistress of the house.

She took good care of the other children and Chiffon, raising them together. All the children became successful and had respect for Chiffon and her mother.

TALE 10

VILASI VINCENT, THE ZOMBIE THAT RETURNED

VILASI VINCENT WAS the most attractive man in Oranger, Bainet. Before he was captured by the vodou priest when he was younger in the middle of the seventies. He was born well-to-do and from the most generous family in the neighborhood. Their house was very stunning, standing on the hill between the fifth and eighth sections. You couldn't miss it wherever you were coming from. The red roof made it even more beautiful.

Family Vincent was a very unique family in the area, for people knew them as Protestants. Mr. James Vincent and Mrs. Amelia Vincent were also prayerful people. Missionaries came from everywhere to visit them. They had a station at the church and at their home where weekly prayer and choir practice took place. They had two children, a girl, Esther, and a boy, Vilasi. Both were in their teenage years. Vilasi was seventeen years of age, and Esther was fifteen. Vilasi was a temptation for every girl in the region.

When this tall man put on his three-piece blue suit, he would look at you with his brown eyes and raise your eyes to look at his gray hair, very well combed. Tell me who wouldn't fall in love with Vilasi. Because of his beauty, his education, and wealth, every parent wished for him to marry his or her daughter.

Everyone in the area knew Vilasi was in love with Hannah Broyer, the daughter of Jacques and Dieula Broyer. Her family owned the largest grocery store in the city of Bainet. Oh god. She was a beautiful dark-skinned girl, and she was a graduate of a renowned school in Port-au-Prince. She was also a Protestant. She had been in love with Vilasi for three years. However, there was a young witch in Oranger who loved Vilasi. Her name was Peninah Préval. Her father and mother were Mr. Constant and Mrs. Asefi Preval. They were known to own a bizango band. Neighbors had to watch the band dance in their home some nights. What happened next was very fascinating.

It was on a hot day. Many young men were swimming in the river and playing baseball with balloons that Bethel's brother brought from him from Port-au-Prince, Some adults brought their horses and mules to drink in the river below them. Vilasi was the best swimmer and a good soccer player, and he was the one with the most experience in volleyball because he was playing volleyball while he was in school in Port-au-Prince. He would always play soccer with the other young men before they went to the river to swim. Usually, girls never swam in that area.

Suddenly, Peninah emerged by the river out of nowhere in a blue denim miniskirt and a bodice top. Since she was very tall, the skirt appeared to be really short. She signaled for the tall, young, princely looking Vilasi to come out.

Vilasi had on his swimming trunks. He looked very muscular but very flat at the same time. He walked away with Peninah, and he was out with her for a while. When he got back, we asked Vilasi, "Did you just have sex with Peninah?"

"How do you know?" he responded.

"We just know. We also thought you must have had sex with her before. Otherwise, she would not have come here and picked you up in your swimming trunks."

"What are you going to do with Hannah?" one of us asked.

"I hope you guys don't talk about this because if my parents find out about it, I'll be in trouble."

"How did you start this relationship with Peninah? When did this relationship begin?"

Vilasi answered, "Last week. I went to buy some olive oil, and her parents saw me there. Mr. Préval told me that he would love for me to marry Peninah."

"Did you tell him that you have a girlfriend named Hannah?"

Vilasi responded, "I told him, but he said to me that if I do not marry Peninah, he will take my zombie to work with him. I am scared."

One of the young men by the name of Bethel asked Vilasi, "Doesn't the Bible say we should not sit with the ungodly? So how did you end up being in a vodou worshiper's home?"

"I was cooking, and I went there to buy some oil."

"And what happened?"

Vilasi said, "I did not see anyone there but Mr. Préval and Peninah. As soon as he finished talking to me, Mr. Préval left me in the house with Peninah. I went to bed with her. Then last night, Mr. Préval called me to say that he heard I had sex with Peninah, and if I do not marry Peninah, he is going to take my zombie."

Bethel asked a very curious question, "Did you tell your mother and father about that conversation you had with Mr. Préval?"

"No, I can't," responded Vilasi.

"You got to go and tell your family right away, or you will be in trouble," Bethel responded to Vilasi. Then Bethel went and told Vilasi's mother about the situation.

Mrs. Vincent placed her hand on top of her head. "Oh God, what didn't he tell me? Vilasi got to sit in those people's houses? Even go to bed with their daughter? I am going to lose Vilasi."

Mrs. rushed to speak to her husband, who was down the hill in the field. Mr. Vincent was troubled. He dropped the hoe; then ran toward his house. He ran after him. They arrived at the home. Mr. Vincent picked up his machete to head to the Prevals' house. His wife held his hand and took the machete and said, "We must pray."

They both knelt down and prayed. They decided not to fight with the Préval but instead would send Vilasi away on the same day to Port-au-Prince in order to spare his life from the vodou worshipers and the bizango society owner.

One of the men in town described to Mr. Vincent, "You do not want your son to get into the hand of the bizango. I was staying in my house at a distance, looking at them dancing at the Prevals. The group is very scary. Those men sing through their noses. They dance like robots.

They dress and look like all kinds of animals. They are so scary. Seeing is enough to kill you."

They packed Vilasi's suitcase in such a hurry. Mr. Vincent saddled two mules, then he asked one of his guardians to drop him and Vilasi in downtown Bainet to pick up the autobus to Port-au-Prince.

The news went quickly to the Préval family that Vilasi was sent to Port-au-Prince in order not to marry their daughter. They both laughed, then Mr. Preval opened the front door of his house so wide, he pointed his machete in the air and said, "I heard somebody is playing with fire around here, but beat the dog and wait for its master."

"Uh, if they'd had known who we are, they would have been coming to us asking for Vilasi to marry Peninah," said Peninah's mother. "Maybe they don't know if Peninah is already pregnant, or they thought we are stupid. They took their handsome son into hiding. Who can hide from the eyes of Ozanfè and our bizango?" Stated Mr. Préval.

In Port-au-Prince, Vilasi has been praying every morning, noon, and before he went to bed in accordance with the instructions that his parents had given him. One night, he had a dream. He saw Peninah come to visit him. She was pregnant. She took his hand, trying to have him rub the baby in her belly. While he was trying to do that, she turned into a large dog and tried to bite him. He was able to hit her with the Bible and said, "I bind you in the name of Jesus!" Then she disappeared. He had a small New Testament Bible. He woke up and read a psalm. The New Testament Bible he always kept in the back of his pocket, but when he was sleeping, he put it under his pillow.

While Vilasi was in Port-au-Prince for about three months, he started going to school. While he was in class one day, one of the students told him that there were two men outside looking for him. He left the class and went out to check. Upon arrival, one of the men threw powder on his face and said, "Ozanfè needs you!" Then he lost consciousness but not completely. He realized that both men had him on their shoulders and took him to a car. He could not talk. It wasn't too long; he heard music, singing, and dancing. He saw that he entered in a very large barrier. When his consciousness somewhat returned, he found himself at Ozanfè. He saw Préval, his wife, and Peninah there.

Peninah turned into a large dog as he saw in the dream. She did not bite him, she sniffed face. Then she turned back into a person and said, "I lost you, but your parents lost you as well."

He kept his head down because he already realized that all the zombies had their heads down. He did not say a word because he did not want them to know that he was still conscious. He was praying in his heart. However, he had not fully awakened. He was living between reality and a fantasy world, so some awareness they did not think he had. He was conscious enough to try to ask the men who picked him up a question, "Where am I?"

But they responded, "You are not allowed to ask questions here!"

The men realized that he was not fully lost his ti bon ange, then they forced him to drink something that put him deeper into a fantasy world. He was praying in his heart. Once he awakened again, he found himself among a bunch of zombies working. There was a ceremony at Ozanfè during that first night he spent there.

Bizango societies from all over Haiti came to celebrate there. As he brought them food that night, many of the bizango men and women wanted to take him with them. They loved him because of his beauty. They asked Ozanfè, "Where did you get this beautiful one?"

Préval stood, "I brought him to Father Ozanfè. His mother and father are Protestants; they thought they were invisible in Oranger. I sold him to Papa Ozanfè."

That night, Peninah was there with her father. She went inside, trying to find Vilasi, probable to hit on him.

Vilasi saw her coming. She turned into a dog and was looking. Vilasi hid and was praying, "God hide me with your feathers. God hide me with your feathers. God, please hide me with your feathers."

One of the zombies came around and hit the dog with a chair. The dog ran and cried. Everybody could hear the dog.

Peninah came back slowly and sat down. When she had to get up to go back with her bizango society, she told them that she wasn't feeling well, but never told her father what had happened. The bizango tried to carry her back home, but before they got to Orange, she died.

When the news came back to Ozanfè that Peninah had died, Ozanfè said to Preval, "I told you to be careful with those Protestants. They are very powerful. They might have done a prayer after her. Don't continue to go after them. You will be a victim. We have one here. That's enough.

The men who came to get Vilasi at the school were themselves zombies but were supervising him and the other zombies. Zombies that were not doing work or were not fast enough got beaten more, but they were never able to put their hands on Vilasi. He was doing his job, and they liked him. However, they were unaware of their actions. Vilasi was not completely subdued, but he pretended that he was as unaware as the other zombies. He was miserable because he worked a lot outside, watching the fields at night. He did not sleep much and worked very hard. His feet were swollen, and he was malnourished.

In Port-au-Prince, Vilasi was staying at the house of his aunt, Sister Emma. After a long time, she had not seen Vilasi; she went to the radio to report that Vilasi was lost. At the same time, she sent a message to Mr. and Mrs. Amelia Vincent to inform them that Vilasi had disappeared from school. They were praying for Vilasi to return, but three months later, Vilasi had not yet returned. She was a woman of prayer. Every morning she woke up, she raised her hands, "God almighty, I know you will bring Vilasi back. He will return to testify the glory of God. Amen Lord! I am waiting for you, Lord. You will promise me that you will never leave me or forget me!"

On the night Sister Emma prayed to God and said that she believed that Vilasi would return, Ozanfè had brought a group of bizango to his house for a festival. All the zombies were working very hard. Vilasi's legs were swollen from walking, standing, and carrying heavy stuff. As Ozanfè was dancing with his wife, all the demons were clapping and dancing.

Vilasi hid behind a coconut tree and began to recite Psalm 118 in his mind. At once, everyone started yelling and running; they felt somebody was biting them. Ozanfè ran; he fell and his right leg broke. The party stopped and was shattered, and the next day, Ozanfè said that a squad of policemen came, but they never saw any men came before and started biting everyone and destroyed the party.

Psalm 118 was the first psalm Vilasi learned by heart.

One day, early morning, Hannah arrived at the Vincents. She told them, "Last night, I had a dream. Vilasi came to me. He said to me that 'I am in the hands of Ozanfè. I always pray to God, and I know the Lord will release me. I will come back to marry you. Your only need to pray for me and read Psalm 118 to ask God to release my soul."

Mrs. Amelia said, "Praise the Lord, I am going to pray, and I know God will return Vilasi because I am his servant."

They prayed every morning and every afternoon; at the end of the prayer, they recited Psalm 118:22 to 24: "The stone the builders rejected has become the cornerstone; the LORD has done this, and it is marvelous in our eyes. The LORD has done it this very day; Let us rejoice today and be glad."

One night, the Vincents asked the Pentecostal church to come to their house for a revival night. They went around and invited all the neighbors to come to the revival.

Préval heard it. She said that he was going to bring his bizango group the same night and early enough for the Protestants to be scared not to come.

Sure enough, the bizango society started dancing and singing at his house, but the Pentecostal came out anyway unafraid. As they began to sing, clap their hands, and prayed a lot, the bizango group saw lightning coming down from heaven. They ran. Some cried. They broke their legs and arms. In the morning, many of them came to the family Vincent to ask to be converted into Protestantism.

One day, a group of missionaries came to the area where Ozanfè's kingdom was. While Vilasi was working in the field with the other zombies, he heard the singing and chanting. He escaped and went to see them. Upon arrival, he knelt down. He told them that he needed prayer.

They made him knelt down on his knees and prayed with him. It was on a hot day. He continued his way with them until he got to a certain place. He told the pastor what had happened to him. The pastor brought him to a marketplace that he knew called Sorèl. He gave him money and asked Vilasi if he thought he could make it home safely. Vilasi said yes. The pastor released Vilasi there and went back to continue his mission.

About three months after the bizango incident, a group of us young men was swimming in the river. This tall and princely looking young man arrived. He looked like someone who was lost. He was skinny, his face was beaten, and his legs were swollen, and he seemed to be unaware of his surroundings. We remembered seeing him in the area before, but he looked very much like a young man that we knew in the area. This other man happened to be his cousin. The man appeared by the river with a florid complexion. We knew that the guy that he resembled had a brother living in Port-au-Prince, and we learned that his cousin who was lost resembled him as well. We thought that, probably, he was the brother or the cousin who had returned from Port-au-Prince. But since we were much younger than he was, we did not ask him any questions. He was kind of recalcitrant. He looked different. He appeared weak; probably, he walked a long way from Jacmel to Oranger, Bainet. Without any embarrassment, he took off his clothes and jumped into the river.

We all began to laugh at him, but he didn't seem to care that we were laughing at him. A few minutes after he jumped into the water, he started a strange conversation. He began to tell us stories about the water, the town, and the people who lived in the area. He said that he thinks he was in the right place, but he could not remember. We began to call him crazy until he told us that he was the son of James Vincent and Amelia. He told us that he just came from Ozanfè kingdom. We did not even listen to him before we all ran and told our parents we saw a zombie in the river because we heard a lot about Ozanfè.

I ran to my house and told my father I saw a guy, but he might be Vilasi that he had been talking about. He happened to be the godson of my father. "Vilasi you saw? I don't believe you. Are you sure?"

"Yes, Father," I responded.

Mrs. Amelia was in prayers, praying for Vilasi to return. As she was reading Psalm 118 with the other sisters who were praying for Vilasi, she came to verse 17 that says, "I will not die, but live, and declare The Lord's works." She began to say praise the Lord and said, "I truly believe, Lord, that my son will not die. His loss will be a testimony for me and the community."

All the women began to praise the Lord with her. Then, someone knocked at her door. "This is Andre. I heard somebody said that Vilasi is by the river."

Mrs. Vincent responded, "I believe it!" Then she ran to the river. The other women ran after her. They did not hear Andre and did not know why Mrs. Vincent was running. One of them yelled, "Did someone say Vilasi is down the river?"

They all continued to run toward the river. Mrs. Vincent jumped into the river with her clothes on and embraced Vilasi. "This is my son," she said.

She sent someone to look for Mr. James, Vilasi's father, her humble husband. He arrived and all of them embraced Vilasi in the river while the whole neighborhood watched in awe.

Everyone in the area remembered him. They recalled how they cried when they heard he vanished. Vilasi explained to everyone where exactly he was for a year, at Ozanfè's. On that day he was picked up, he was unconscious for a period of time, then he regained full consciousness, but neither Ozanfè nor the guardians who worked for Ozanfè realized Vilasi regain his consciousness. He learned the name of the two zombies that picked him up: Constant and Asefi. He said those two zombies were very obedient to Ozanfè; he trusted them and sent them out for major missions to capture souls around the country.

To Vilasi, sometimes he felt his disappearance was a dream, other times it looked like it was real, but it was a reality that two zombies came and picked him up at school, and they brought him to Ozanfè.

He now realized how people still kind of feared him, thinking he was a zombie and that he had the power to bite them. His godfather came to visit him after he learned that Vilasi reappeared in the area. He came in front of Vilasi. Then he stood there. He was scared to death. He made a cross's sign with his right hand.

"In the name of the Father, the Son, and the Holy Spirit," he prayed heartily. Vilasi was standing against a sycamore tree.

My father looked straight at him. He took a deep breath. He looked right and left. Vilasi folded his arms across his chest, maybe to tell my dad, "I am safe. I won't hurt you." But my father almost backed off.

My mother said, "What are you doing, Andres?"

I remembered thinking; *I thought my father was braver than this.* Then he walked toward Vilasi. "Vilasi, is that you?" The way he asked Vilasi the question, made Vilasi scared. My father is a strong man with a big chest. He never went to the gym, but he looked like someone who had done weight lifting.

The tall Vilasi did not respond. Vilasi turned to look at his mother as if to say, "Do I know you?"

The question brought tears to his eyes.

The mother said, "Yes, you are my son, Vilasi. I remember your wide eyes that made every woman love you."

Vilasi moved toward his mother to hug her. She ran. She got scared. Everyone laughed.

"I am okay, Mom!" Vilasi called after her. As Vilasi testified in the church one day about what the Lord had done for him and how Peninah turned into a dog, trying to come after him while he was at Ozanfè. God made another zombie hit her with a chair, and later, he learned Peninah died that day.

He saw Mr. and Mrs. Préval came forward, knelt before Vilasi, and said, "Pray for us. We are going to accept your Christ."

He prayed, and they became Christians.

Vilasi was still one of the good-looking guys in Oranger. As someone said, "Oranger never produced ugly people, and God has been with some of us too."

He was partially confused, but he seemed to know what was going on. Everyone was looking at Vilasi as if they were dreaming.

A woman said, "Oh, look at his curly hair. If he is looking for a woman, I will marry him."

"Shut up!" Another young woman yelled. "This is a serious matter!"

Vilasi looked at me. He smiled. I was one of the teenagers who first saw him by the river. He signaled to me to come to him. I turned to look at my dad.

"Go ahead." My father signaled to me with his head. Then my father said, "I am going to stay close in case he tries to harm you."

I gave him my right hand. I said hi brightly. He kissed my hand. He held me. Then everyone realized Vilasi was real. They moved toward him. Everyone tried to give him something with salt to eat to see if he would eat it.

One of the women said, "He is not a zombie. A zombie does not eat salt."

Vilasi looked at everyone and laughed. He said, "I am okay." He spoke, "While I was at Ozanfè's, I knew everything. Ozanfè had complained that he was unable to take my *ti bon ange* (little soul). Ozanfè also asked me about my background as Protestants because, every time he went to bed, someone came to his dream and told him that if he does not release me, he would die."

Vilasi continued, "Ozanfè said, 'I hope Constant comes to get his demon here before he destroys my kingdom. He has too much power for me.'"

How did Vilasi disappear? Vilasi gave us a testimony on what happened.

"I was in love with Hannah. Everyone in the area knew about the relationship. I went to buy some olive oil. Chez Constant and Asefi arranged with Peninah so that I could get her pregnant. Since they knew that my parents are Protestants, they thought I would marry Peninah if she got pregnant. When my parents sent me to Port-au-Prince, they thought that they lost me. The Prévals went and sold me to Ozanfè. After Ozanfè sent them a message to let them know that he had me in his possession, they went to pay, and then Ozanfè told them that I was too strong for him. I have too much power. At night, I prayed. Many of Ozanfè's zombies had left. He gave me back to Constant and Asefi. While I was coming back with them, I was tied up in chains, but the River of TiPen was so strong. Both Asefi and Constant went to the sea. I felt someone cut the chains, and I was released. Someone took my hand and crossed with me to the river. After I crossed the river, the person disappeared. I know it cannot be anyone else who rescued me. It is God of heaven."

The day before Constant and Asefi went to pick up Vilasi, he had a dream. In the dream, he found himself in heaven. Vilasi told us that in heaven. He played with the hawk; they sang with him beautiful songs. "I did not know that animals can talk, but in heaven, they talked."

He and the animals understood each other's language. He slept on top of the wild snakes, and they had done nothing to him. He hid under the yucca, nothing happened, nothing whatsoever. He felt great in that heavenly place. His master was there in his imagination, but he wasn't there physically for him to touch, see, smell, but he could see his footprints and hear his voice.

"I heard him driving his chariot, and then I saw his back as he went by. It was great listening to God whispering in my ears. He is a loving God. He is the only one who is alive among the gods. I saw in heaven how angels watch over us. I believe he would save us from dying too if we do his will."

In the dream, Vilasi wished he stayed there forever. At first, Vilasi did not see anyone in heaven. He walked alone in the garden of God, alone in the wide garden. He said, "Everything in heaven is made of gold." While he was walking in the garden, Vilasi saw an angel at a distance. "Can you help me, sir?" he asked the angel.

"What are you doing here? No man is supposed to be here in the garden."

Vilasi looked at the angel and said, "What about you, sir?"

"My name is Cherubim. I am in charge of this garden."

"Can I stay with you?" Vilasi asked the angel.

"I do not know. I don't have control over the garden," the angel replied to Vilasi.

"Who does?" Vilasi asked the angel.

"God does!" the angel replied. The angel took him on a tour of heaven. He passed near the throne of God. He saw angels there singing a beautiful song. "Our God is king. Our God is king, King of kings forever and ever."

He thought to himself, "*These angels are happy. I will never leave this place.* At once, he woke up and found himself in the kingdom of Ozanfè. He saw Ozanfè standing in front of him, whispering to his face.

In that kingdom, no one slept. Everyone was crying day and night. He cried to God, who created him, to save him from the hands of Ozanfè. He would like to go back to the dream of being in heaven where he had not encountered any difficulty in that beautiful heaven in which he emerged. But it was too late for him. Vilasi was beaten daily by Ozanfè; they gave him all types of things to drink so that he could become a zombie, but he was never able to transform into a zombie because his parents and Hannah were praying daily for him. Ozanfè had no power over him.

One day, Ozanfè prepared a yearly ceremony at his home. Vilasi saw many animals beginning to arrive, mostly dogs. One of the dogs began to look at him. The dog advanced and sat close to him. Another dog began to sit next to him. Then both dogs began barking at him. Ozanfè right away realized that they were jealous of Vilasi.

The ceremony began. Most of the drinks were homemade, mixed with blood. Most of the meat was made of human flesh. Some of the goats and cows that Vilasi and the other zombies were taking care of in the field were humans that were turned into animals. There was lots of music during the ceremony. They began to dance. The animals were moving around. For the first time in his life, Vilasi saw dogs singing and dancing. The voices were like music.

> Whoopee, whoopee, whoopee,
> Hoop, hoop, hoop,
> Whoopee, whoopee, whoopee,
> Hoop, hoop, hoop, whoopee,
> Whoopee, whoopee, hoop, hoop, hoop

They were hoping to get Vilasi, not to bite him but to dance with him. They could have torn Vilasi up. Every one of the women in the ceremony would like to take a turn with Vilasi. One of the dogs turned into a young woman. The young woman walked toward Vilasi. She began to touch Vilasi's curly hair.

"No, that is unacceptable here," Ozanfè said to the young woman. "I do not allow living beings to play with my zombies."

"That's too bad. I love him, and I want him," the woman replied. The woman, according to Vilasi, was very powerful. Once she touched Vilasi and tried to put her hands in his pants, she got electrocuted.

"Oh, this man is a demon! He burned me!" she cried to Ozanfè.

Ozanfè responded, "I have no control over him. I am waiting for his owner so that I can give him back to him. If I leave him here, he is going to destroy my kingdom."

Vilasi was a dispatcher of Ozanfè. Due to his good looks, Ozanfè sent him to places to attract women, as well as men. He was welcomed wherever Ozanfè sent him. Since Ozanfè was very rich, Vilasi could eat whatever he wanted.

According to Vilasi, one could not do anything wrong when residing in Ozanfè's kingdom. One had to follow the norm that was set by him. One, it was not allowed to go to bed with zombie women. They would beat him if he was caught. While Vilasi was testifying about how God delivered him from Constant and Asefi, the news came to Oranger that Peninah's parents died at TiPen while they were trying to cross the river with a zombie named Vilasi. Vilasi escaped, and they died.

TALE 11

DADDY, I HEARD MOTHER SCREAM LAST NIGHT

I T WAS RAINING very hard outside at the end of October in 1973. It was when hurricane Flora began to cease. It was only 8:00 p.m., but 8:00 p.m. in the provinces was considered late. My father was coming home when he saw something spectacular that stood at the back of the house. It looked like a helicopter. The thing opened its wings; it brightened the entire house with splendid lights.

Since the rain was so heavy, my father wondered, "What is a helicopter doing at the back of my house? This is very peculiar because no one had seen a helicopter in this area before."

My father was very scared; his children and his wife were in the house. He must advance to see what that magnificent thing was. He moved closer. He saw the thing shake both its wings. He looked closer. He saw the feet. The thing is a biped. He saw the hands under the wings. My father looked closer. He saw the face of a woman. The thing had not seen him, but it smelled him. The thing moved on its back like an airplane, trying to take off. It moved forward and backward and tried to fly a few times, but the rain was too heavy on its wings, and it was too dark. My father moved closer to make sure he could describe what he saw. He was so fearful, he urinated on himself. He looked closer.

"Is this mother? It must be her," he said to himself.

Before the thing saw him, he hit his machete against a dried palm branch on the ground. She screamed and flapped both of her wings and flew toward Grandma's home, and Dad heard the thing fall hard on the ground. My father could see the thing's wings hang against the palm trees. My father leaned against the house to watch. He finally saw the lights turned off and were no longer able to see the wings, and he opened the door and went inside the house as he still held his machete firmly in his right hand.

As father entered the house, Mario told him, "Dad, I heard Grandma scream."

"Go to bed," his daddy said.

Dad could not sleep for the rest of the night. Early in the morning, he woke up and went down to Grandma's house. Upon arrival, he saw Grandpa standing on his large and beautiful court filled with daisies, lavender, and daffodils. Usually, Grandma was in the kitchen making coffee and getting breakfast ready for everybody.

My father asked Grandpa, "Where is Mama?"

Grandpa answered, "She is in bed."

"What is wrong with Mama, Papa?"

"She is in pain."

Grandpa looked down to the ground. Dad saw a lot of blood. "Where is this blood coming from, Papa? Did you kill Mama?"

"Oh, son! What are you saying? Do you know me as a murderer?"

"Sorry, Papa, that is not what I meant."

"Is Mama all right?"

"I don't know what is happening to her. We went to bed last night. She was okay, but this morning, I saw her bleeding. I asked her if everything was okay. She said yes, but she is in a lot of pain. And I see a trail of blood from the field to the room."

Dad ran to the penguin trees. He saw where she fell. She bled a lot there. *How did she make it home?* Dad questioned himself as he looked at the place where Grandma fell.

"Why did you go over there? Do you know something?" Grandpa asked Dad.

"I do not know anything, Papa, but Mama should tell us what happened to her," he replied. Papa ran inside the house. Grandpa ran behind him.

"Can I go in, Papa?"

"Of course, son, this is your house and your mother's."

My father asked her, "Mama, what is happening?"

Grandma pretended that she was sleeping. Dad tried to turn her; she screamed. Then Dad saw multiple places where she stung by the penguin all over on her side. Grandma said to my father, "Get out! Demon! I don't want to see you at my house!"

Grandpa was suspicious. "Tell me. What did you do to her?"

"Dad, how can you ask me that? Didn't you say that she went to bed with you last night? And she wasn't bleeding then, was she?"

"I would say no. We had a good time before we went to bed last night." Grandpa knew that Grandma had been accused as a witch before. He just came from the law with her last week. A mother accused her of scratching her son's hand, and the son almost died. The judge made Grandma give the child medicine, and he was healed. Grandpa looked at my dad. "Is your mother-in-law really involved in witchcraft?"

"I don't know, Papa."

My father looked in the bed; it was filled with blood. My father said to Grandpa, "Hurry. Let us take her to the hospital. She is going to die." Then Grandma lost consciousness. However, after many days in the hospital of Bainet, she recovered. When she came out of the hospital, she asked my father, "Whom did you tell?"

My dad answered, "About what?"

"Did you do that to me?"

"What are you talking about?" my father asked Grandma.

"Nothing. Forget it." Grandma convinced herself that it was not my father who scared her.

I went to many vodou temples with my father. I have many insights about my encounters with vodou rituals. With my own eyes, I had seen men perform supernatural acts before me. I can give you some good examples. I recalled a time when I came from Port-au-Prince to Bainet to see the family. There was a woman who happened to be a close family member. I always called her Aunt Gertrude, but I am not sure if she was my aunt or a friend of the family. I never remembered to ask my dad. I had to leave for

Port-au-Prince again the next day. I said to Dad, "Please, Dad, take me to Aunt Gertrude. She offered me some money."

My father said, "It is late now."

"It has just turned seven o'clock, Dad. It is not too late."

"Son, six o'clock here is very late, but I will take you. We are men. We cannot be scared to go out."

My father and I arrived at the house around 7:45 p.m., and in those areas, it used to be very dark around that time. He had to walk in the midst of the bananas, coffee, and cacao trees. Upon arriving at the house, my dad touched me; he tried to whisper, "Look! Be quiet!"

We saw a woman on her back, hovering like an airplane at the back of the house. She went back and forth, back and forth. Then her wings came out. I was frightened, but my father held me and said, "Do not fear." Then we saw her straighten her legs and fly. We noticed her legs behind her, her arms were under her wings that looked like those in an airplane. She traveled very fast and descended.

My father said, "That's Gertrude. She went to perform her witch duties. We can go back home. She is not there." My father was calm. He said to me, "I am not surprised. I experience these things all the time."

I wanted to make sure that was Aunt Gertrude. My father went into her house through the window, and then he opened the door for me. We saw Aunt Gertrude's skin wide open on her bed. "Don't ask me how she took it off," my father said.

"Yes, this is the way they do it. They transform into something else. They can kill you if they know you see them. When she comes back, she will smell us. She will know someone came to her house, but she is not going to know who. I could throw the skin away, and she would die a few hours after the demon comes out of her, but I am not going to touch it. Never tell anyone you came here, and if she finds out, she will kill us."

Another time, my father caught Grandma again at the back of the house. She was getting ready to fly. My father had his machete in his hand; he hit it against the wall, and then she got scared, flew down to the next house, and began to yell as if something had hit her. My father yelled to her, "I never want to see you at the back of my house again, or I will cut your head."

All the neighbors heard her. They also heard my father talk to her that night. The next morning, she did not say good morning to my father until she died many years later. She and my father never said hello to each other again. They became enemies after that encounter. She also hated my father's children.

Grandma became sick. I heard everybody say that Grandma was going to die. I said, "Dad, can you take me to see Grandma?"

"What do you want to see her for? She is not too sick to eat children," my dad responded.

We, as children, were not allowed to visit her. In the Haitian culture, if someone with the witchcraft spirit becomes ill or dies, the demonic spirit still lives after the death of that person to torment family members from one generation to the next.

One morning, someone called my father to tell him Grandma was about to die. No one covered her face. My mother and aunts were afraid to see her dead. My father ran down and entered the room. Without the consent of her daughters, my father stained her eyes, and he said to us, "She can never follow you again. I did everything I am supposed to do."

I still do not know, besides blotting her eyes, what else my dad had done.

During her funeral, my parents called each one of us, children, to cross over her body three times. Three days after the funeral, I sat by the river with many other children playing on the sand. I must tell you though I was the one she hated the most, but I can't tell you why. I saw Grandma. I told the children, and then I tried to get up to run. She put pressure on me; I was numb and unable to speak any more, and then she crossed my head three times. I went and told my father about the experience, but he did not believe me at first.

"Son, your grandma is dead. She can't persecute you anymore. Besides, she has no eyes."

About a week later, we all were sitting in the courtyard. My father was present at the time. I saw her coming toward me. "Here is Grandma, Dad!" I said.

"How do you see her? What type of clothes is she wearing?" my father asked. I explained to my father that she wore the old dress, which she used to wear when she was alive. She used to wear a long dress with red, white, and blue on it. My father said, "Go touch her."

I tried to get up. I couldn't; she was pressing down on me, and I could not talk. My father tried to talk to me. I was numb. She crossed my head three times and left. Then I was okay.

This happened to me for almost a year. Sometimes, once I lay down in bed, I'd see her coming. Until one day, I was sitting with my mother in her courtyard, and then I saw Grandma coming. I said, "Mother, there she is. Grandma is coming to cross over my head."

My mom said, "Where is she?"

I said, "Right here."

My mother had a red handkerchief; she pulled it out and gave it to me. "What is she doing now?" my mother asked.

"She is backing up," I said.

My grandmother began to back up. She was afraid of the red handkerchief for some reason. Then my mother told me she was going to stop my grandma. She sent me down to call my father.

My father told me, "I am sorry that I did not believe you, but you will never see her again."

Ever since my father made that promise, I never saw my grandmother again; later, they explained to me what they did.

Another time, I went on vacation from Port-au-Prince. The first day was a wonderful day. My brothers, my sisters, and I went to the beach and enjoyed the day. At night, it was rainy. My father woke up very early as he is used to. Then we heard him crying, "Oh! Oh! Oh!"

"What is going on, Dad?" I asked. I ran down to our field. I saw my dad with his mouth wide open. "Are you okay, Dad?" I asked.

"No, son! The thieves took twenty plantains. They also took one of my pigs. They took advantage of the rain. It must be somebody who knows that I don't like rain because they know I may not come out last night."

While we were talking, a friend of his arrived at the house. "What is wrong with you?" he asked my father.

My father told him a thief came to the field last night. "I lost twenty plantains, one pig. This is what I know. They might have taken more."

"Oh! You have this problem, and you never told me. I could have them stopped a long time ago. You are my friend. I have nothing to hide from you, the same way you have nothing to hide from me."

"I am a member of a *bizango* group. I can stop people from stealing from you."

Bizango is a group that walks at night. They also eat human flesh and take people's zombies. He told my father that he could bring the group to dance at the house, and after the dance, people won't steal from his field because they would believe that he belonged to the *bizango*. This is the most frightening demonic group in Haiti because they eat human flesh.

My father came and explained to us that the group would be coming, but we did not have to be scared. The group wouldn't harm us. Between eleven thirty and midnight, I heard a noise of songs from a great distance. They came and entered the house. They danced nonstop for about half an hour. First, I did not want to go out. I was afraid to come out because many parents turned their own children in to those groups for money. My father said, "You do not have to be afraid. They won't do anything to you."

Then I decided to see what was going on. The scene was amazing. A woman came to my father, gave him a kiss right on his lips, and then she became a white dog. She jumped up and then smelled everyone as a real dog would have done. She then became a living human being again. She laughed and then became a huge snake. I really don't like snakes; I tried to run, but my father held me to stay. The woman now turned into a female cow. She walked back and forth in a circle and turned again into a human.

She embraced a man then began to dance. She then became a young woman, and the man changed into an old man. They danced for a long time, then both of them turned back to themselves, then my father went to embrace the woman and shake hands with the man.

"Wow! This is amazing," my father told them. Then my father handed the man a bottle of wine. Around two thirty, they left. I went to bed and could not sleep after experiencing the power of man.

Another story that my father told me and I do believe it because I have seen the power of vodou in Haiti. When my father was young, his father used to smoke a lot. He always sent my father to buy tobacco three to four times a day. One day, he was about to send my father to buy him tobacco. My father said to him, my grandfather, "Dad, I am not feeling good. Can I go buy it tomorrow?"

He answered my dad, "I want it now!"

My father said, "I really can't go, Dad!"

He said to my father, "I am going to count to four. If you don't go, when I die, you will not participate in my funeral. I won't let you." He continued, "I will make you cry and throw stones. People will think that you are insane. They will tie you up until my funeral is over."

My father laughed, and then he said to Grandpa, "When you die, you are not going to know anything."

Grandpa answered, "We will see."

Once he died, my father began to throw stones at people. He became mentally mad. They had to tie him until the next day when his father's funeral was over. As soon as the funeral was over, he calmed down. He did not even know about the death of his father until after the funeral.

One of my aunts was a big vodou worshipper. She had this vodou spirit that used to mount her almost daily. This spirit possessed her during her sleep and took her out. She flew everywhere without knowing what she was doing. Every morning though, when she woke up, she was tired, had body aches, and was sleepy. She knew that she went to bed early. She wondered, *What is going on with me?* She got caught when one of her grandchildren got sick.

The son-in-law went to a vodou priest, and then the vodou priest told him that his mother-in-law was doing something wrong to the child but that she was unknot conscious about her witchcraft. The son-in-law tried to tell her that, but she cried and said that she was not a witch. The son-in-law asked the vodou priest to help him make her aware of the vodou spirit. The vodou priest told him that he could do that.

One day, after my aunt went out after the ceremony, she could not go home. She then realized that she had been going out at night, and she already belonged to a witchcraft group. Her husband said that he realized that she was going out at night because she began to sleep during the day, and many nights, he woke up and he found her crossing him, trying to put him to sleep before she went out, but he never told her he knew about it. She cried and began to tell everyone that the spirit taught her how to be a witch. She was the only one on my father's side of the family that became a witch during her vodou manifestation.

She died with regret because she never wanted to come over to Protestantism before her death. When my father explained that to me, I went and offered Jesus to my aunt, but she told me that she could not accept it because the vodou spirit would have killed her.

After I converted into Protestantism, there was a demon spirit behind me wherever I went. The spirit used to appear by the fence whenever I was going out. She had many rings on her fingers. She wore dark glasses and was dressed in black, and her mouth was rosy. She used to stand in the middle of the road and say, "You can't pass unless you kiss me." She would give me a big kiss, and I would feel her, but I could only see her face in my dreams.

Once I converted to Protestantism, I would say to her the verse of Matthew 4:10. That was the only thing that I had to say, then she would run away. I did not have to say the word; once I said the verse, she would run away. Whenever I was taking a shower, she showed up and touched my private parts. I wouldn't see her, but I would feel her. Then she would come at night in my sleep to tell me that she visited me. The first time that I encountered her with the spirit was when I was very young.

I went to the beach with my mother, brothers, and sisters. Then I saw her coming toward me. What a beautiful woman she was physically! She took me and went to the water, and none of the people there saw her. She kept me in the water for a long time. She touched me all over my body and gave me a shower but did not harm me. She spent too much time with me in the water. I became very sick and could not talk afterward.

My parents were looking for me for a long time before they found me. I used to see her whenever I was taking a shower or in my dreams. Whenever I saw her, I said Matthew 4:10. Then she would leave.

One day, I met with the spirit in my dream. She took me by the neck. I took her by the neck also and said Matthew 4:10, "Get away,

Satan! For it is written, 'You shall worship the Lord your God and him only shall you serve.'" This was what my pastor told me to tell her when I see her in my dreams again. She burned. I heard a voice that said, "I have never seen any man so powerful. You will never see me again." That was it. The devil left me ever since. But one thing that I learned, vodou spirit never leaves you. The spirit stops visiting you whenever you're close to God, but if you stop praying, the spirit returns to torment you and your family members, and thus, it goes from generation to generation. So the best place to be is on Jesus's side.

Vodou, in my experience, is a satanic religion. This is a religion that if one follows it, a man can become a homosexual, and a woman can become a lesbian. People can become thieves and killers. Vodou is very powerful. It causes people to become a drunkard, immoral, blasphemous, a sorcerer, delusional, a pervert, and it brings poverty to people from one generation to the next. For example, I knew some people in Haiti who were not allowed by their vodou masters to send their children to school. They became slaves to the snakes in their homes. They had to be washed in clay, washed in hot water, danced in fire, and had sex with animals. For these vodou powers to leave a person, one must completely surrender to Christ. Therefore, the vodou spirits would remain with the person wherever the person went until the person made a public confession that he or she would not serve those vodou gods anymore.

A person who is possessed by a vodou spirit received his or her power from the heavens, the earth, under the earth, the water, the seas, and the sky. I met many women who told me that they became sorceresses during their sleep by the loas that mounted them and made them fly at night, eat all sorts of reptiles, including, snakes, mice, etc.

The best thing to get the vodou spirits out of your way is not to give it access and leave the vodou habits completely, including lying, stealing, and rebellion, and wearing improper clothing. One should also go to a good church where the pastor knows how to pray and break the vodou curse. If you give it access, it owns you. He can pick you up in church while praying if he wants you to serve him. He is very powerful.

TALE 12

JESUS SAVED ME FROM DEATH

I WAS ABOUT THREE years old when I was sick with a cyst on both sides of my neck.

Uncle Apilus had a ceremony for the vodou gods at his home. This was a ceremony in which Uncle Apilus always invited all the gods (loa/lwa): Ogou Feray, Ogou Badagris, and even Simbi Dlo, Erzulie Freda, and Danto. The dance took place in January 1969.

A woman overcame by the vodou spirit took a black pig, placed it on her shoulder, and walked with it back and forth while she was singing, "Jean Petro, you called. Jean Petro. Here I am. Ti Jean Petro, if they don't give you your black goats and black pigs, you eat their children."

He slapped another man. Then there was a fight between the two spirits—a man who was saddled by Ogou and another by Ti Jean Petro. Ogou Feray was so angry; Uncle had to give him strong black coffee to calm him down.

A few minutes later, he cut the throat of the black pig, drank some of the blood, and sprinkled the rest on the attendees. Then he walked toward my father. He took my father by the throat and said to him, "I am Ti Jean Petro." (Ti Jean is a fire loa who lives in the bushes. He is a powerful magician who primarily deals with black magic, and he's part of secret vodou" [Wikipedia]). "I want you to give me a pig just like this next year."

The man who was saddled by Ogou had calmed down long ago, and the vodou priest said that he left because he did not want to fight with Ti Jean, and he would come back once Ti Jean left.

My father glanced at Ti Jean to make sure that Ti Jean was not looking at him so he could leave the ceremony. Ti Jean turned his face and realized my father was trying to leave, he angrily said to my father, "I will harm you or your children."

I stood there and looked at him with hatred in my eyes. She pointed at me and said, "You are the one that I have chosen."

My father was scared but said he would not bow down to Ti Jean Petro (a vodou god). My father did not believe that the woman was possessed with the spirit. He, therefore, never offered the sacrifice. It was about a year or two later, a cyst began to grow again on both sides of my neck.

My parents were scared. Many people believed that Jean Petro put the curse on me. They asked my father to offer food to the loa so that I would not die. My mother went to a town called Lunette to consult a vodou priest (Ougan) as was the practice of most Haitians.

My mother asked the priest to call the spirit for her. According to my mother, the man put a white bucket full of water under a chair. He did everything that he was supposed to do and then told my mother he saw a man coming toward him. The man was hairy. His face looked like the face of a man, but his mouth looked like that of a pig.

My mother said, "Call him."

The man arrived and identified himself to my mother as Jean Petro. He told my mother that he was a family member from my father's side. He was handicapped. He couldn't go to places to find food as the other vodou gods would. My parents had to sacrifice a pig for him, or he would kill one of their children, whomever he chose. He said to my mother that he lived in the forest, water, seas, and the skies and that his powers allowed him to fly on air, and if need be, cause terror to human lives. He could force the government, as well as individuals, to fight against each other. He said that he sometimes made people angry. He destroyed many families. He could manifest as a man or a woman whenever he wished so that he could attract people.

My mother asked him that since he was so powerful, why was he looking for a black pig?

He said that he did not eat from everyone but only from the people he chose. He did not want food from my mother but, rather, from my father. But my father chose not to feed him; for that, he was going to harm me. My mother cried. She thought that I was going to die, but I was still here, giving glory to God, the most high, and to Jesus, the king of kings, who delivered me from that world of darkness.

One thing that I know, there is a God. I must serve him and do his will. I have experienced him in everything, in dreams, as well as in real life. I was very sick at a very early age. My parents had no way of saving me. I had a cyst on my neck. The cyst was very large.

My family took me to a general hospital, and the doctor said to my parents, "I know it is hard for you, but I don't think doctors can do much."

A nurse said, "Oh, such a beautiful child with brown eyes."

Another woman said, "Only Jesus can help since he never rejects any cases."

I turned and looked at her face, and I smiled at her nice words. And my parents could not do anything themselves. They felt helpless. The doctors suggested that we find some other hospitals where there might be American doctors who had experience with major surgeries.

We went to St. Francois de Salle Hospital. While I sat there, I spoke in Jesus's ear. The doctor requested that my family take me to a place called Fond-Des-Blancs. I went to Fond-Des-Blancs where there were white doctors, but they were not Jesus. They smiled at me. They had pity for me. They could not do anything for the poor boy.

I was very lucky at St. Francois de Salle Hospital; my sister suggested that we go to the cathedral to pray to the saints before we go farther in our destination. God sent an angel to wait for me there. At the cathedral, we found a woman standing by the church.

"What is wrong with this child?" she asked my sister. My sister told her that she did not know exactly what was wrong with me, but most people thought that it was a vodou loa on my father's side that caused the cyst. The woman replied to my sister, "Do you believe in God?"

"Yes," my sister replied.

"Well, that is all your brother needs. Vodou has no power over him. Vodou spirits can only control people who follow them, but they don't have power over people who don't believe in them." The woman had pity for me. She asked me, "How do you carry your neck? Is it heavy?" I had some suspicion that the woman was an angel from God. "Do not fear, God is watching over you," said the woman. She told my sister that there was a hospital in Fermathe called Wallace Hospital. She said if I go there, they will find a solution for my neck. My sister took me to Wallace Hospital the next day.

I love my brother Paul, my cousin Cayetan, and my sister Melanie. I felt bad that my sister Imacula died. They did a lot for me.

They all went to the hospital with me. Wallace Hospital did an X-ray and told my family that my condition was too grave. "Take him to Grace Children Hospital right away! It is located at Delmas Thirty-First," said the doctor in charge.

They took me to Grace Children Hospital on the same day. All the doctors looked at me and were amazed.

"He won't survive," one of them whispered in the back, but I could hear him.

"What is wrong with him?" they all asked.

"I have never seen anything like this," said one of the doctors. They realized that they could not do anything for me; the doctors sent me back home.

While we were leaving, a woman walked toward us and said, "Fear not. There is nothing Jesus cannot do. Trust him. He is an omnipotent God."

They told my family that they did not have enough beds, so they could not keep me. They said that they would call me as soon as a bed became available. Less than a month later, a bed became available, and they called for me to be admitted to the Grace Children Hospital.

I was admitted to the hospital in February 1972. I left in March 1973. I was still sick. The cyst did not leave my neck. In the hospital, I met two fourteen-year-old young men, Henry and Julio. They were young, but the power that they had in Christ Jesus was incredible. When the three of us prayed, Satan fell to his knees.

I met a girl named Marie Michelle who memorized most of the psalms. With her, we prayed daily. We talked to Jesus like friends. He listened to us, and we listened to him. The doctors realized that they could not do anything for me, but I still didn't understand why they did not refer me to Jesus at the time. I met Jesus then, but I did not know him fully. They called my parents to pick me up.

"This young man has been in the hospital for eighteen months. Every doctor who comes here refused to even consult him. We had one of the best groups of doctors who came from the United States last month. They looked at him and said there is no hope," said Dr. Thea.

Once I got home, I became sicker. My sister was getting ready to send me to Bainet. She thought I was going to die. Bainet is the city where I was born, a city of witches and vodou worshippers like all the other cities in Haiti. Jesus is also alive in some Christians there. My parents were ready for the funeral; they bought white pants, shirt, and socks, but Jesus had a different plan for me. I thank God for Grace Children Hospital.

They could not give me life, but they gave me two bibles that taught me about Jesus as my lord, king, and savior. I prayed that God bless the employees there; they took good care of me. They taught me how to pray. They taught me how to read the psalms. They taught me to love the Lord with all my heart. I could never forget Mother Jean (Manman Jean), Ms. Daddy, and Gizelle. How could I ever forget Papa Michelle, Gesner, and Reno? I also love the missionaries. They spent money to put that hospital in that poor country. The hospital saved millions of children, including me. God bless each person who had given his or her money to that hospital.

The only reason that those missionaries could support a hospital like that was because they allowed God to use them. God lived within their hearts and gave them his understanding.

I pray to you, Lord, to bless those who thought to build that hospital.

My sister Melanie went shopping; my aunt Gania was selling goods at the market. My brothers, Louis and Michael, and my sister Marie went to school. I was left alone in the house. When I was leaving the hospital, I was given two bibles, one in my mother's tongue and the other was in French. I was also given a little book called *Coeur de Jacques*. It is translated as *The Heart of Jack*. I was not interested so much in the Bibles but *Coeur de Jacques*. This little book was full of pictures.

While I was reading the little book, I was looking at the movement of the pictures. I hope I could find this little book again. Jacques was a man who was living a filthy lifestyle. Jacques did things that were unpleasing to God. Jacques became a Christian and realized that he could not do filthy things anymore, but he must live a life where he had to offer his body as a living sacrifice to God. Now, all the animals and the reptiles began to leave as Jacques became more and more sanctified, and all the animals and reptiles that represented Satan left Jacques's heart. I was about thirteen when I was admitted to the hospital, but I was so little, people thought I was ten.

After looking over the pictures, I prayed like this, "Dear God, I would like for you to clean my heart. Give me a heart as pure as Jacques's heart. I know that, Lord, I am a sinner, but please forgive me so that my heart can be as pure as Jacques's heart."

God heard my prayer. Jean Petro heard my prayer too. On that same night I prayed, I had a dream. I was going to heaven. I met many rich people on the way. They offered me money to work for them. I said to them, "I am going to heaven to see my God. I don't need your money or your jobs. In heaven, I will find everything."

I continued on my way to heaven. I also met a man who told me, "I will give you everything that you need. You will enjoy life better if you follow me."

"I chose Jesus already," I replied in the dream.

The man showed me all the money he wanted to give me. He showed me a beautiful house. "I am going to give you that if you follow me."

I went inside the dwelling, and I met with Lucifer. He introduced himself to me. While Lucifer was talking to me in the dream, I heard people crying. I turned right inside the empire, and I saw many people that I knew. They were tied with chains. I looked at each person's face; I released everyone I knew and said to them, "Let's go to heaven." I said to Lucifer, "I am taking those with me to heaven to meet with Jesus."

He tried to catch me, but he couldn't. I was in the midst of a wild wind.

"I don't need your money or anything that you can offer me. I'd rather have Jesus," I said to Lucifer and took off with thousands of people behind me.

Lucifer tried to follow me to heaven, but he could not touch me. There was a wild wind that was blowing him and his army back.

In the dream, I arrived in heaven. I saw a man at the palace, and I asked him, "Do you know where God is residing?"

"Who is asking for him?" the angel asked.

"I need to see him," I replied.

"Nobody can see God unless he has the heart of Jacques," the man replied.

"I have the heart of Jacques. I can see him," I replied.

"Go over there," the angel told me. He continued, "Weigh yourself on this scale, then it will allow you to go through if you weigh appropriately."

"What is the appropriate weight?" I asked the angel.

"I am not in the position to tell you," the angel replied, "but the scales will tell you."

I went up the scale. I weighed myself. Then a gate opened wide for me. Then the angel pointed to me where God was. He said, "Go, but your friends can't go! God will tell you if you have to come back to pick them up."

I went and saw God. He was a short man dressed in dirty blue jeans. He looked like he just came from the fields. He had a machete in his hand. In my heart, I doubted. "This can't be God."

He looked at me as if he understood what I said. Then he transformed into this most handsome, tall white man that I have ever seen on earth. Then I looked. I saw angels dancing and singing like they were inaugurating a new president. I also saw some resplendent children who came to play with me. I loved the children, and I loved the temple too.

God took me by the hand like I was his little child. He walked with me through the entire temple. He began at the back of the temple all the way to the altar. Then he showed me a chair on the second row, on the

JOSEPH P. POLICAPE

right side of the temple, and he said, "This is where you will be sitting." He lifted up the chair, he showed me a white robe. I had never seen anything so white. He showed me a golden crown. "This shall be your crown. Go back to earth. Fight for it. I have lots of my children that will look up to you to take them to heaven. Make sure you bring every one of them to me, young and old. Do not be afraid. I will be with you."

He said to me, "It isn't time yet. You asked me to give you the heart of Jacques. I gave it to you. Go work with it."

I said to God, "I don't want to live on earth any longer. Earth is heartbreaking. The place is bad. It is not for me," I replied.

God said, "Do not let Jesus hear you. He will be angry. He went through hell so that you could come here."

Then I looked, and I saw Jesus looking at me. I bowed my head and saluted him. He said to me, "Listen to my father."

Then God handed me a penny in the dream. "This penny is worth more than all the money the rich men and Lucifer offered to you on your way here. Take it with you. Share it with everyone around you."

I looked at the penny. In my heart, I said, *what can a penny do for me?* The children looked at me and signaled for me to take the penny. I looked at the children and refused to take the penny. To me, the penny was too small. The children looked at me a second time and signaled for me to take the penny from God. God handed the penny to me again for the last time.

"Share it with your friends. The more you give from it, the more I will bless it." Then God also spat in my right hand and said to me, "This is my peace. I give it to you, my joy and my grace. Anyone who stands against you, I will also stand against him. Whoever blesses you, I will also bless him. You've been blessed because on earth, there are not many boys like you who want God."

Then God called a dog to come to bite me. I called my friends who were with me, and I said, "Let's go!" I ran and fell into a gigantic river.

I was awakened suddenly. I felt better after I prayed. Then I fell asleep once again, and I had another dream. I could not eat for a long period of time after I got back from the hospital. My throat hurt. My mouth could not tolerate anything, not even water. I could not talk. I was ready to die. My tongue was infected. The pain was unbearable;

I preferred death over life then. I recalled what my aunt Gania told me, "I know that you are going to die, and you know it too, but you are a very strong boy. I need you to pray to God. Tell him, 'Dear God, I am going to die, but I want you to take my soul. Please do not look at my mother's and father's sin, but look at me as who I am.'"

Once she left, I knelt down. I closed my eyes and began to pray. "Dear God, I know that I am going to die, but please take my soul to your kingdom. Do not hold me liable for my parents' sins, but look at me as an individual who wants to follow your status."

At once, I had a vision. I saw a big man walking toward me. The man was hairy. He had a man face. His mouth was like the mouth of a pig. The man put his hand around my neck and tried to choke me. He said, "How dare you think that you can be a Protestant in the family. Who is in your family that is Protestant? I am going to kill you because you refused to serve me."

I said to the man, "In Jesus's name, you can't do anything to me." I could not talk before, but then my tongue relaxed. I gained strength and began to pray. I looked, and I saw a white man coming toward me. He had a long beard. He was dressed in a white robe. He was smiling, and he looked as bright as the sun. He carried a long knife. He touched my neck. He shook his head, and he said, "You have faith."

He put his fingers on my chest and said to me, "I am going to heal you, but it is because of your faith. I never had seen any child with your faith before. You heard that the Bible talks about a boy named Samuel. He never had your faith. I am Jesus. I am here to heal you, but it is because of your faith." He said again, "Continue to love God with all your heart. As long as you continue to love God, nothing can ever happen to you on this earth. I will send my angels to walk with you as long as you live.

"Go tell people what your faith has done for you, and many will come to believe that there is a god that controls the universe."

The man took a knife and cut both sides of my neck. He took two huge glands out from each side of my neck. He showed me the cysts that he took from both sides and said, "Touch them." When I touched them, they were very hard. The man said, "Nobody could operate on you but me." The man hugged me, and he left, and as he was leaving, he looked back at me with a great smile on his face. He said to me, "Keep your faith, and you will see the glory of God."

I woke up from the prayer. I did not know if I was healed. My brothers, sisters, and aunt came back home and I told them about the experience. My brother Michael came and saw that I was healed. On that same night, I went to church and testified what God had done. "Praise the Lord!" Also that night, I had a dream. I saw the woman I met by the cathedral. She told me, "You remember I told you Jesus could heal you."

Still today, my only prayer is that God gives me the heart of Jacques. I could be in jail, but if I have the heart of Jacques, I will be victorious. People may accuse me of anything they wish, but for me, I know that I have the heart of Jacques, and I can't hurt other people. I can't criticize other people, and I will serve my dear Jesus as long as I live. I pray to God almighty in the name of Jesus, who was nailed on the cross and resurrected on the third day, and in the name of the Holy Ghost. I must do the will of my God until I leave this earth.

TALE 13

ATHENA AND HER WORLD

I F THERE WAS a feminist movement in our world, it started in the country of Haiti with Athena Polo, whose maiden name was Bruno. She was born with a distinctive and independent personality. She grew up to be an elegant dark-skinned five-feet-six-inch-tall woman with long brown hair. When she opened her mouth, every man fell in love with her. She was a great communicator. However, it was very difficult at first to identify her as a man or a woman. She wore an invisible mark to make it impossible for people to know who she really was.

When Athena wanted to be among men, she dressed and behaved like a man. When she wanted to be among the ladies for her advantage, she dressed and behaved as a woman. Some women said, "Athena was born to make a difference in this world and in vodou, which she considered as 'a lewd religion.'"

One of the students from her school said, "I suspected that she was a girl. We all called her the dandy guy, for she was too beautiful to be a man, but she was not afraid of darkness and knew how to handle chaos. She was a strong-minded person, and physically, men were afraid of her, for no one knew what she could do. She was brave."

Athena was the daughter of Papa Seidon, as everyone called him. Papa Seidon was a monster killer in Pétion-Ville. He was best known as a zombie-taker, snatching the souls of people. He also was known as someone who could turn into any animal he wished. He was a well-known vodou priest in Pétion-Ville. He considered his daughter, Athena, hard-nosed, for she refused to accept his ways.

Papa Seidon never knew that Athena was against his religion and his way of life until Papa Seidon found out. He was ready to perform his annual vodou ceremony where he was going to burn dollars, kill seven black cows and as many black goats, pigs, and chickens as the vodou gods asked him. He was also going to take the stars from the heavens as he used to do every year, and many people were going to watch the spectacle of his family dancing under his temple.

His wife was going to turn into a snake and into an eagle and fly with her daughters on her wings. Papa Seidon dressed up; his wife dressed up and was ready to leave with his three daughters. He purchased one bag of many colors called in Haitian Creole, *macoutezacha*, for each of them. Each daughter was supposed to wear her blue jeans and dress of tricolors—red, white, and blue stripes. He put a bottle of hot pepper in each bag, a bar of soap, and wine. Each woman wore a red bandana, tied on the right, called *mare an clodinèt*.

Joanne and Rachel were ready to go. Papa Seidon called, "Where are you, Athena? It is time to go, we are late. The dance can't start without us."

Athena came out, "Daddy, who told you that I am going to continue to attend your vodou ceremonies? I am sick of following something that I dislike. I can't wait to grow up. I would not want to deal with family members who are involved in this lewd, dirty religion."

Papa Seidon could not believe what he was hearing, so he asked her, "What did you just say, Athena? Ogoun is dirty? Marinette is dirty? Baron Samedi is dirty? The dead will kill you, Athena. You are rude, Athena!" Papa Seidon continued, "Al mete rad la sourou, Athena! M ba wtwaminitavan m craze w (Go put your clothes on, Athena! I give you three minutes before I break you)! Ah . . . Athena, ou pa bezwen swiv mwen ankò? Outrò gran fanm (Ah . . . Athena, you do not want to follow me anymore? You are too big of a woman)!"

Papa Seidon continued, "I don't tell you not to become a Protestant, but you can't abandon Agwe, Erzulie, Papa Legba, and Pedro. These are the gods of your ancestors. They are the ones who protect us."

"Daddy, if your gods have the power to protect you, why can't they feed themselves? Every year, you have to kill animals to feed them. Once I saw them mounting you, I see you go wash yourself in clay like pigs. Sometimes they put you on fire and leave you. If people were not there, you would have burned to death. They call you their horse. You are not an animal, Daddy. Only gullible people serve such gods. And, Daddy, this is the reason you sent your daughter to school, to see what you could not see.

"Now I see that there is a true God in heaven. You can't see the true God. I have decided that I want to follow the true God, but you have decided that you are going to follow the little dirty-feet gods. If my sisters want to follow you, they can, but I won't anymore."

"Okay, Athena. Map kite w, map voye Papa Legba vinnchache w (Okay, Athena. I will leave you. I will send Father Legba to pick you up)."

"Okay, Dad. That's a good way to see it. I will see the power that I received from Jesus of Nazareth and that of Papa Legba which one is stronger. If Papa Legba can come to get me to go worship him, I promise you, I will stay with Papa Legba for the rest of my life. But if Papa Legba does not pick me up, I will stay with Jesus as long as I live."

"Oh, Athena, how many times have I asked you not to mention that name? Every time you mention that name, you put me in trouble with Papa Lucifer. All the spirits leave the house."

"You mean the name of Jesus, Daddy?"

"Oh! Athena, you do it on purpose. Lucifer will kill me, and he will kill all of you in this house when we have to meet with him tonight. If you mention that name tonight, Lucifer will fall on his stomach. This is not going to be good for you. Okay, Athena? This is the reason I do not want you to follow the Pentecostals."

Athena answered, "Daddy, this is a real reason for me to follow Jesus. First, you just testified that his name is powerful. If his name can put Lucifer on his stomach, he deserves to be praised. Second, I do not know about you, but I am going to heaven, and Jesus is the only one that can take me there, not Lucifer, not the false gods you serve."

"Oh, Athena! You say I am not going to heaven? Is this what you wish for me, Athena? God is your god. He did not create me?"

Athena responded, "Daddy, I think you are confused. Everyone is not going to heaven. Do you want to know who is going to heaven?"

"Tell me, Athena!"

"Well, Daddy, this is what the word of God says, to go to heaven, you have to love the Lord with all your heart, with all your soul, with all your strength, and with all your mind, and you must love your neighbor as yourself." Athena did not let him answer. "And, Daddy, I know you are going to tell me that you love the Lord, but if you miss one of the above I just told you, you can't go to heaven."

Papa Seidon was thinking a little bit. "You know I love the Lord, and I love my neighbor."

"Daddy, if you love your neighbor, what about all these zombies you bring to the house all the time? Those people that are working hard for you in the fields, they are people you killed. They are your neighbors."

"Oh! Athena! You talk to your father like this? You're a curse. Did the pastor tell you to come and tell me this? Did you tell your godmother and your pastor I have zombies?"

"No, I have not told my pastor or my godmother about your zombies, but Jesus knows you have them here."

"Oh, Athena, don't mention that name here. Also, I never want to hear anymore that you tell me that you are going to see your godmother. She is a demon. I tried to kill her, but I can't. That woman is on her knees every day, but now she has poisoned you, Athena." Papa Seidon continued, "Ah, Athena, you will force me out of business."

"Ah, Daddy, if Jesus's name has all this power, you should get out of your vodou business to follow him. You will be in peace. My mother will be in peace. My two sisters that you delivered to Satan will be in peace."

"Athena, even Father Henry will be at the ceremony tonight. Do you think you know more than Father Henry who went to school for seven years to become a priest?"

"Dad, going to school to become a priest doesn't make anyone right with Christ. To be right with Christ, each one of us needs to have a relationship with Christ. I have no right to tell you that Father Henry is not going to heaven, but the Bible tells me he is not going because the Bible says, 'If anyone is in Christ, he is a new creation. All things are passed away, and behold, all things will come anew.' I see Father Henry here all the time, consulting you to give him magic. He is part of your *bizango*. Therefore, he is not a Christian."

"Oh! Athena, you mean everyone who goes to the cathedral is not a Christian?"

"No, Dad, I did not say that. I said if people go to the cathedral and at the same time worship Erzulie and come to consult you instead of God, they are not Christians. God can do everything, and he knows everything. His followers would not consult a vodou priest to help resolve their problems. My Jesus is a great mathematician. He can solve every problem."

"Oh! Athena, don't mention that name! If you continue to live at my house, you must respect my house. From now on, you are not going to church. Athena, tonight, I am going to see how much power you have. Let's go, everybody!"

The entire family went to the ceremony, but Athena stayed in the house. Mrs. Cézanne, Athena's mother, looked at Athena with apologetic eyes "Your father will kill you. I don't care if you die. I will cry, and then my tears will dry."

The father was very angry because this was a night when vodou priests from around the country would be there, and some had traveled from around the world to watch Papa Seidon's power. There would be a contest with all the witches of the world. He wanted to show his wife as the most powerful witch in the world. The two daughters, who had been trained on witchcraft, each would go on their wings, and she would fly with them. Then she would meet Lucifer in the air with a glass of blood before he descended to earth for the ceremony.

The ceremony began. Everything went according to plan, but once Lucifer came down, he asked, "Where is your third daughter? Athena is her name?"

The papa said, "Athena doesn't listen to me. She wants to follow that man. You know who I am talking about. I can't mention his name."

Lucifer got mad and left the ceremony; while he was flying back, he said, "When you have Athena here, call me. I need her."

The father was embarrassed before all the visitors. The ceremony was a defeat for Papa Seidon because of Athena. Papa Seidon, while inside the party, turned into a pig and left temporarily the ceremony angrily. He was planning to kill Athena. Before long, Papa Seidon arrived at her door.

Athena was inside, on her bed, sleeping. Once he arrived, Seidon turned into a demon. His arms got bigger. He turned into a monster; he performed his secret, and the door was wide open while Athena was sleeping. He tried to touch Athena. His entire right arm got burned. He yelled and then ran out. Athena knew nothing of what had transpired.

When Papa Seidon arrived at the next ceremony, he was all burned. His face was filled with blood. His right arm was completely burned, and his legs were broken. When the witches saw him, they all ran. His wife and daughters took him to the hospital.

Athena woke up and found the door open. She thought she left the door open by mistake. Then the mother came with the daughters. Athena asked for her father; the mother said that the father was in the hospital, but the father never told them what happened.

Athena went to the hospital to see her dad. "Dad, what is happening to you?" Athena asked her father.

Papa Seidon responded to Athena, "You are a demon! Please leave the hospital right now. I have nothing to do with you. You are a murderer!"

Athena responded, "I am not a murderer, Daddy, and I will never be one."

He said to Athena, "You will pay for what you did."

Athena left the hospital. The family was not happy with Athena. She lived in the house in fear of what could be done to her.

The father returned from the hospital. He did not care too much about Athena, but he asked her not to go to church ever again. Papa Seidon was a very strong man, well-known, and a rich vodou priest. He sent his three daughters, Athena, Joanne, and Rachel, to the best school in Haiti, but Joanne and Rachel could not stay in school because vodou gods had selected them to serve in vodou temples. Every time they went to school, the loa mounted them in school and took them back home.

One day, Joanne went to school, and a girl who rarely talked came up to her.

The teacher said, "Joanne, go to the board."

She got up and went to the blackboard. Then she began to dance with her neck going back and forth, back and forth. She was mounted by a loa named Dumballah. Then she ran and plunged into the pool of the neighbor. Then a neighbor ran and gave her an egg. She cracked it open and drank its contents. She began to clap her hands; she raised her dress on top of her head and began to swear. She told the boys, "If you want sex, here it is."

The teacher said, "I have no control of this one anymore."

She was all wet. She went back to the class, then she became like a snake. She was able to go under every chair in the classroom.

It was different for Athena. Before she went to bed every night, she prayed. When she is leaving for school, she puts her knees down to pray, "Jesus, I believe in all your promises. You promised that you will not leave me alone. I pray that you watch over me. You are everything to me. I do not trust anyone on this earth, Jesus, you are my savior and my king, and I put all my confidence in you." Then she would go to bed or leave for school or wherever she is going. Whenever she went out, the father sent zombies to follow her and to try to kill her. Athena never knew anything.

The zombies reported to the father that they saw an army surrounding Athena. The father one day went by himself. He saw Athena in the midst of an army of men and women who were well-armed. He got scared and returned.

Sometimes, when Athena was sleeping, he tried to go near her door, he got electrocuted. He did not know what do to with her. When Athena was eight years old, her godmother took her to church. She converted. Since then, every Sunday, she went to spend the weekends with her godmother, then she went to a local Baptist church with her godmother. On the other hand, since Athena's sister was very young, Joanne was chosen by Zacha, and Rachel was chosen by Agwe; many times, the spirit took Rachel to the sea. Sometimes, her parents thought she would die because she would be in the sea for hours then come back while she was singing, "Agwe, Agwe O, nan letan m te ye (Agwe, hey. I am Agwe. I was in the sea)."

At a very early age, the two younger sisters became vodou priestesses, but there was no vodou spirit that could mount Athena. Papa Seidon could not understand why Athena was able to stay in school, but the other two couldn't. However, he realized Athena was not too interested in his vodou dances. When Athena was young, a vodou priestess predicted that Erzulie had chosen Athena, but she could never mount Athena.

Athena would attend for her parents' sake, but she would stay at a distance. Finally, Mr. Seidon decided to stop sending the daughters to school because they could become stronger than he is in the vodou temple, but for Athena, it was different. She was outstanding in her schooling.

On November 1, Papa Seidon began the vodou dances. He went down by himself because he knew that the loas would go pick up each girl and the mother to bring them down. As soon as he left, the two sisters began to whistle and to sing vodou songs, and they would go down to the dance. The mother, Cézanne, said to Athena, "Hurry up! Your father is waiting for us down there."

Athena responded, "I am not part of your ceremony. You must leave this darkness of vodou. There is a plain light of Christianity out there. God did not create me to serve false gods but rather to adore him."

The mother responded, "I regret that I am going to lose you because I know Erzulie never plays. You will die, but what can I do? I will bury you."

Cézanne began to dance up and down as she was going down the hill.

One day, while her parents and sisters were dancing in the vodou temple, Athena joined her godmother and went to the local Baptist church. She saw her parents as deviant figures who preferred to choose Satan over God. She left the world of vodou to live in a world full of hope that she called the Christian world.

The father, while at the vodou dance, met a young man named Servile, the son of one of the vodou priests named Jano, who came to celebrate with him. The guy is twenty-seven while Athena was fourteen.

Seidon told the young man while they were sitting in the darkness, waiting for Lucifer to descend, "I have a beautiful daughter. Her name is Athena. Would you like to marry her? She wants to be a Protestant, but I am sure you are going to make her the reign of your *bizango* band fast."

Papa Seidon was going to marry his young daughter Athena to him. When he got home, he said to Athena, "Ah! I found a rich man for you." Once Mr. Seidon entered the home, he saw Athena sitting in the living room, studying. "Oh god, look at my beautiful girl! Darling, I found a handsome and rich man to marry you."

Athena looked at him and responded, "Daddy, I hope you do not say that I disrespect you. I am a child, but you should see that I don't want you or anyone else to tell me who to marry, what religion I should follow, how many children I must have, or what level of education I should receive. The God who created me will direct my path." Athena continued, "God tells me in his word, 'My father and mother may abandon me, but he will take care of me.'" Athena said again, "From now on, I am no longer a girl. If I were a boy, you would not choose men to destroy my reputation."

Papa Seidon was surprised to hear Athena speak to him like that. "Ah, you have a mental problem, Athena." He smiled. "Come in!"

"Daddy, I have no mental problem. I am a child of God. He has a plan set for me."

"Okay, Athena, you started this. I promise you, Athena, this is the last time you are going to talk to me like this. You will die, Athena."

Athena did not respond. She went straight to her room, went down on her knees, and prayed to her father in heaven, "God, I know my father will try to kill me, but I pray that you, Jesus, who I choose to serve you, raise me up in the midst of all evil spirits. Then I want to see one day my father glorify your name for me."

From that day forward, her conviction that this change in her appearance would save her life had her dressing like a man, but she still had a voice of a woman, so she had to train herself to lower it. Everyone who did not know her before this masking was confused whether she was a man or a woman. She wanted to stay as such because she believed that as a man, her father, would have more respect for her and that she could get what she wanted—a good education to live a better life in a man's world or "a vodou world," as she called it.

To get her way, Athena began to wear pants and told people who didn't know her that her name was Salomon. However, her parents knew they had a girl named Athena, not Salomon; but if she called by her name, Athena, she wouldn't get too far, and thus it was that way everywhere in Haiti. Women were discriminated against then. Besides, parents could marry them with whoever they wished; they could not hold most of the positions that a man could hold in society.

Not only in the area of Pétion-Ville, Athena was not only the most beautiful woman, but she was also the well-taught girl in Port-au-Prince. Her two younger sisters were already married and had children but did not go too far in school. During her era, there weren't too many scholarly women. Men used to believe that women were inferior to them. If women were to go to school, they did not go too far in their education. Women were believed to be weak in math and sciences, so they were encouraged to marry early, stay at home, and take care of the children.

Athena had more male friends than female friends. Men would come to Athena's home daily after class to study. However, when they invite her to go to a party with them, she said, "I am a Christian. I can't go to parties where there is alcohol and dance. I wanted to be different from any other woman who grew up here, and if I have to be a male for a while, that is fine with me. I did not want to be dependent on men, and if this is the only way for me to know what is out there, and if I must imperil myself to achieve my rights as a woman, I must do so. Many people would say that I am a bad woman, but sooner or later, many of them will realize why I took this route. Not even my sisters understood or knew the real situation."

Her parents never slept at night. They worried about their daughter. They lost trust in her because she went her own way and made her own decisions.

"My daughter would never find a man to marry," the mother used to say.

"You put yourself in peril by camouflaging as a man. If men found out that you are a woman, they will rape and then kill you, or no man will ever marry you," said Papa Seidon.

"I am not looking for a man, Papa. I want a man to look for me, and if he loves me, he would never want me to be a housewife, and when it is time for me to be a female, I will be. I also will be a good wife for a man without being his slave," said Athena.

One day, Rachel found Cézanne crying at the back of the house. "Mama, what's going on?"

"You know what's going on. You don't even have to ask me. Athena will never marry to give me grandchildren like you and Joanne."

Rachel answered, "Mama, what have we got from marriage? You and Dad destroyed my life and Joanne's. Now I know why Athena refused to marry. I am better. I still have my husband with me, but Joanne's husband had left her with two children, and besides, if I were the one to choose my husband, I would not choose the man you and Dad have given me. Eventually, I will leave him too."

Cézanne could not believe her ears. "Oh, Rachel, it is what you have kept in your heart to tell me?"

"Yes, Mother. You and Dad destroyed our lives. Now Athena is like a man. She did that because of you."

Cézanne answered, "Oh, Rachel, I am going to Saint-Antoine. I know Saint-Antoine would give me my justice."

Early the next morning, Cézanne went to Saint-Antoine. "Oh, Saint-Antoine! Father, I know you have power. I ask you to change my daughter. Oh, Papa Legba, Mommy Erzulie. I have no other to call, but you to help me with my beautiful daughter who is completely crazy. Let her know that she is a female and that she needs a man in her life for her to become a woman of prestige. What am I going to say, oh, Saint-Antoine, if my daughter loses her innocence?"

After Cézanne completed her prayer, she had a dream. Saint-Antoine came and arrested Athena. Early in the morning, Cézanne offered food to the loas. "Oh, thank you, Papa Ogoun. Thank you, Mama Erzulie, Mama Agwe for changing Athena for me."

But Athena was not looking for a man; she neither wanted to worship Erzulie, whom she hated, nor obey her parents in that circumstance. She was looking for a good education and did not want to be associated with their vodou gods. Therefore, her will was stronger than any god that existed in nature. She also wanted to prove to her vodou world that women had the potential that a man had with the help of God.

JOSEPH P. POLICAPE

A woman could be good in math and sciences just as a man. The only thing the woman had to do was to learn and practice math and sciences.

Athena got up every morning. Instead of cleaning the house, preparing the coffee for the vodou priests and the guests that used to come to the house every morning for her father to predict their future, she went to study math and sciences with the young men at her school.

"Athena, what do you think the neighbors would say about us when they see our young girl sitting in the library, studying with young men?" Cézanne asked.

"Mother, I don't care what my neighbors have to say about me. In fact, I am not a girl. I am Salomon. They don't know what I am looking for, but I do. I don't want to be a man's slave when I grow up. I don't want to serve your loas either. I want to make a difference. I would like to work with men as partners, and when I marry with one, I want him to treat me as his partner, not his slave," responded Athena.

Seidon looked at Athena. He laughed. "Where would you find a man to marry you with your perception, Athena? You are finished. If you can marry, a dog can marry too."

"Marriage is not the end of everything, Dad. If I am married, I am married. If a man decided not to marry me that would be fine with me. I just want to be free because God created me as a woman, but that doesn't mean I have to be somebody's slave," responded Athena.

Seidon turned red. He walked like he was exercising in the army. He went back and forth, and then he looked up and said, "How am I going to stand in this community if Athena loses her virginity?"

Cézanne responded, "You asked me? What if she gets pregnant? People in this town will laugh at us. They will say we do not know how to raise our own children."

Joanne wasn't too far; she heard them talking and said, "You already married two of them. They were all younger than Athena, but they have no future any longer. I do not want you to do the same for Athena. She should be married when she can. If she doesn't find a man of her choice, she will be better off staying without a man. Men don't give life. Both Rachel and I will end up without men in our lives. You destroyed our lives, and I don't like that vodou you put me in. Look how clean Athena is. Rachel and I, we always smell."

"You are a public disgrace, Joanne!" replied Papa Seidon.

"I know that, Dad, but I prefer to be a public disgrace than to accept the marriages that you have given to me and Rachel." To Athena, Joanne continued, "Athena, you have done the right thing." Then Rachel took Athena's hand, and they left the parents sitting on the balcony.

The time came for Athena to go to her baccalaureate, the first woman to ever go to a baccalaureate in the country. However, the school did not know that she was a girl because her name was Salomon Bruno. About six thousand students went. Usually, it was about a quarter of the students who would pass. The exams took place. About three weeks later, they began to call those who passed the exams in alphabetical order and ranking them from one to six thousand. The first ten students would receive scholarships to study abroad, and they would be called first.

Athena was very anxious, thinking that she was going to hear the As then the Bs. The first name that was called was Athena Bruno. The caller stopped and said, "Athena Bruno laureate as number 1 over six thousand students."

She received the highest mark of the entire student body in the country. The men had great respect for her. She was the best in math, sciences, and Latin. They began to ask her for help in those subjects, and she was willing to do so.

After Athena graduated from high school, she went to study law in France. When she got back from France, every business wanted to hire her, but she felt an obligation to work for the government. Then she began to dress as a female again on the job. In spite of Athena's efforts, every time she went to work, men asked to go to bed with her. She told a man one day, "I earned my respect to find a job without having to sell my body to a man, and I won't do it."

Most of her friends could not believe it when they saw her dress like a woman. "What is going on, Salomon? Are you now a woman?"

Athena had to explain to them why she used to dress as a man. Papa Seidon was still worried about his daughter getting married, but he was afraid that his daughter was not a virgin anymore. He currently hated Athena on one hand, but on the other hand, he appreciated what Athena had realized as a woman in Port-au-Prince.

He met a man at an annual ceremony; he went with the other vodou priests again. He and the man became friends. Oscar was the man's name. While he was talking to Oscar, Oscar said to Papa Seidon, "I am looking for a woman to marry. Can you help me find somebody? I need a good woman."

"You are a vodou priest. Every woman wants you. What is going on? Why have you not married?" Papa Seidon asked him.

"I have more than one hundred, but I still need a woman to be my wife, one who is not the same as those I have. I need a woman who can read and write to work for me when I am not there. I have lots of people coming to me. When I receive letters, I have to take them to other people to read for me because I can't read myself."

Papa Seidon responded, "I have a girl I can give you. She can read well, and she can write, but she may not be a virgin. Her name is Athena."

Oscar responded, "Who is she? Who is her family?"

Seidon responded, "She is my daughter. She never listened to me, but now she is getting old. She wants a man."

Oscar responded, "I will never say no to you. You know that. Give me the girl."

Papa Seidon right away described to Oscar his daughter. "She is more interested in school, and she wants to be a Protestant, but I do not worry about that. I am sure you can fix that, but I would like to see my daughter marry a good man. She is a wonderful girl. Don't be afraid. You are going to have a good wife," said Papa Seidon to his associate.

Papa Seidon was very rich. Most men were happy to marry his daughter. He was able to burn over thousands of dollars each year to pay his debt to the vodou gods. He had lots of power around the country. He was a well-known vodou priest in the area of Pétion-Ville.

He went and told his wife about the man, but had not informed his daughter. He wanted to give her a surprise engagement. He invited people from all over Port-au-Prince and the area of Pétion-Ville to come to the engagement ceremony. The man brought his folks, and they came with a nice gold ring. Finally, on the day of the ceremony, Papa Seidon told Athena that he found a man who would love her, and there was going to be an engagement party on that day.

Athena responded, "Sure!"

Then people began to arrive at the ceremony. They called Athena to come, and the man's parents began to talk about the type of woman they would like to have for their son. The father said, "You know, Oscar is very popular. He already has ten children, but he wants a woman who can be his wife. We are lucky she is coming from the Bruno family, one of the greatest families in the country."

While the ceremony was going on, there were some rooms in Papa Seidon's home that were never opened. Athena had a suspicion of what was in those locked rooms. She found the keys and began to open the rooms. In each one, Athena found zombies tied up in them. These were zombies, according to Athena, who refused to work for her father. He put them in jail. In some of the rooms, zombies were sitting and knitting dresses, others were making shoes and pants while others were counting money for Papa Seidon. Athena gave salt to the zombies to eat, and she opened the doors.

Zombies are not supposed to eat salt, or they would be able to come to a normal mental stage again, and they would not stay. Then Athena pretended that she wanted to attend the ceremony, but she already packed to leave the house. She went inside where the fiancé's ceremony was being held. She looked at the people and smiled. Everyone stood up and clapped for her. She said, "Is this about me?"

"Yes, my darling," the father replied. He was trying to introduce Athena to the people. "This is your woman," he told the man, and he pointed at the man. He pulled Athena toward him. "This is a nice man I found for you."

Athena looked straight into his eyes. "Did I tell you that I wanted to get married?"

Papa Seidon said to the people, "Don't worry. She is afraid to get married, but we have to give her to someone. She will cool down." Papa Seidon thought he finally stuck Athena with a man.

Athena went to her room; she called one of her best friends by the name of Liné to bring his to pick up her stuff. Liné was one of the deacons in the church who knew exactly what Athena had been going through. Athena went to her room and packed her clothes. Once Liné came with the car, she stayed behind the wall and dropped her stuff one by one to Liné. Before Athena had left the house, there were two rooms in the house that she never saw her dad open. She wanted to know what was in the rooms. She took the key from her dad's pants. She opened the first door. She couldn't believe her eyes. She found ten zombies, men and women, counting money again inside the room. Once they saw her, they put their heads down.

Athena threw salt at them, and then they began to run. Athena quickly opened the second door. It was filled with a huge snake. Athena shut that door and walked slowly through the hallway, hoping no one would see her leave. As Athena was preparing to leave the house, some of the zombies made it outside before she left. Liné saw one coming toward him. He got very scared; he thought that Papa Seidon saw him and released the zombies. One of the zombies tried to get inside the car. Liné locked the door and started the car. On her way out, Athena left a note for her father and said to him:

Dear Dad,

You have been talking about public disgrace. This is one you created for yourself. Don't think that you have a daughter named Athena anymore. You will not make me go to the cemetery to throw food to Legba. Legba has eyes. He can't see. He has ears; he can't hear. I will spend the rest of my life serving the God above who created the heavens and the earth. Good-bye!

Signed: Athena

Before Liné moved the car, Athena arrived. He said to Athena, "Hurry! Your dad release zombies to get us."

Athena said to Liné, "I did that."

Liné asked Athena, "Did anybody see you?"

Athena answered, "Your sister, Erzulie would have seen me, but she is blind."

After Liné dropped Athena at his house, he said to her, "Both of us are single, and we have the same faith. I propose to marry you." He handed a ring to Athena.

Athena answered, "I am very pleased that you are interested in me, but I appreciate you as a friend. I want our love for each other to continue to be platonic. I am not ready for marriage."

Oscar though was a vodou priest, but he was learning from Papa Seidon how to turn people into animals. Seidon told Oscar and his parents and everyone else who was there at the party that Athena decided not to be part of the engagement and that she left his house. Seidon did not realize yet that his zombies were let out. Everyone was busy. Papa Seidon and his wife were embarrassed, and it was a public disgrace in Pétion-Ville and in the entire area of Port-au-Prince. People in the neighborhood were upset about what Athena had done to her parents, and they thought Athena was not going to survive. However, many families who knew that Seidon killed their sons and daughters and took their zombies were delighted when they heard that zombies escaped from Papa Seidon.

One of the men said, "I know that Athena does not like her parents to choose a man for her. I agree with her. She is a professional. Why should she marry a vodou priest? I would not marry a dirty vodou priest either, but she should remember that Seidon would take her zombie and marry the zombie with Oscar. She will not be able to escape that."

Athena left, and her parents never heard from Athena again, and they did not want to know about her. Not only did she destroy their reputation in Pétion-Ville as zombie owners, but she also did not want to go their way.

Later, the town heard the story of Prince Parker Polo, the richest man in Jacmel, and how he was looking for a wife and how Athena came into his purview and was stricken by her. Prince Parker Polo owned businesses and houses all over Haiti. In Port-au-Prince, he owned houses at Bourdon, Pétion-Ville, and Thomas Saint. He was very rich. He began to search for a woman for his son, Prince Parker Polo Junior. They were looking for a woman with a specific résumé. They searched for the woman in Port-au-Prince; most people thought that what they were looking for would be very difficult to find. They were looking for a woman who was a virgin (this was their highest priority) and beautiful (beauty was their second priority).

They wanted a woman who had completed high school and went to college. The person would have to speak French fluently and know Latin because the family was very involved in international affairs. It was almost unfeasible to find a woman with such a great résumé in the world. In Haiti, that was almost impossible because not many women were very educated then.

Athena was working for the National Palace at the time as minister of foreign affairs. To find a job in such a milieu then, one had to be very educated as a woman to even get inside there. Some of the men were asking Athena to go to bed with them.

Athena lied to them, saying a vodou power from her parents prevented her from having sex with men. She was a woman, but she had a penis, and that the loa spirit that her parents served would kill any man who tries to have sex with her. The word went out so quickly in the National Palace that Athena was not a woman. Every man was scared of her; however, she was too qualified for her job for them to fire her. Then they left her alone because they were afraid of vodou.

To help Prince Polo find a woman, the government sent a letter to every leader in every city, borough, and section to find a woman with the above qualifications for Prince Parker Polo. They spent about six months searching. Every province and city in the country and those who resided in Port-au-Prince sent girls. They spent six months in the capital in beauty treatments. Whoever the beautiful girl found to fit would become Madame Polo or Princess Polo. They found five hundred candidates, including Athena.

It came to pass that about five hundred people went to the competition. After careful review, Athena became one of the last one hundred candidates; then she became one of ten candidates. People at

Pétion-Ville who heard the news thought that Athena was insane to think that she could become the princess of Port-au-Prince, but once they saw her on television and in newspapers, they sent the news to Athena's parents that she was living in Port-au-Prince and that they saw her name in the paper and on television as a participant in the competition. She made it to the last three candidates. At last, she was found to be the only woman in the world with those qualifications.

Prince Polo married Athena, and she became the princess of Port-au-Prince. One of Seidon's neighbors said, "Athena is a woman of the superego. I can't believe that a woman spent all her life with all kinds of men, especially those from Lycée Pétion, and then she still got married a virgin."

He said, "There is a true God, and when he is watching over his people, even death is afraid of them. Seidon killed anyone who disrespects him. Only the god of heaven could protect Athena."

Finally, the long ordeal was over; Athena was declared the princess of Port-au-Prince. Papa Seidon was stunned. He burned all his vodou gods and went to the local Baptist church that Athena used to attend; he converted with his wife and his daughters and their children.

Athena heard that; she called for her parents to come to see her. Upon arrival, her father knelt down and said, "I need your God."

She was thrilled to see that her parents accepted Christ. The entire city of Pétion-Ville brought flowers and palm branches to come to congratulate her and listened to her father testify that he was no longer a demon, nor his wife a witch. Jesus had changed their lives.

Athena raised her hands toward heaven and said, "I thank you, Lord!"

TALE 14

DIANE, THIS IS NOT MY SKIN

WILLIAM THOUGHT HE was in a dream when he saw the roof open wide and a bird as large as a helicopter appeared, flying through it, and the roof closed again as the engineer had made it.

It happened in December of 1957, a few months after Francois Duvalier (Papa Doc) became president. That helicopter was his wife, Diane Boudreaux, the deaconess of the Notre Dame de Bas de Gandou. The small, shy, beautiful, and well-educated woman that he trust and appreciates is a witch, and now he realizes that she is the one who ate all their five children.

How can that be? She works very closely with Father Gerard, the priest at Notre Dame de Bas de Gandou. Every service, she takes communion. Every little sin she commits, she goes to Father Gerard to confess, but she never told Father Gerard that she was a witch like most of the women in the church.

William ran outside to see how high the bird could fly. When he saw the height of flight reached by his wife, he trembled. It was a night of thunderstorms and rain. In fact, early on that day, the news had forecast that all airplanes were grounded due to bad weather.

Diane Boudreaux had to fly to Puerto Rico that tonight, but the weather refused to cooperate; however persistent, nothing could really stop her when it came to her time to attend a ceremony, especially when the program was already scheduled for the last sacrifice of the year, the December ceremony.

The story begins like this. In Gory, Bainet, there was a man named William Boudreaux. William was a dark-skinned six-foot-tall man with brown eyes. He and his wife, Diane, were well-to-do. Both William and Diane serve at the Notre Dame de Bas de Gandou. They were the most educated members of the cathedral and were very close to Father Gerard.

Father Gerard was a well-known priest in the area. He did not encourage witchcraft, but the church was located in an area where everybody was Catholic, including the thieves, the adulterers, and witches. Catholicism was just a cover to do more evil after confession on Sundays. Everybody knew that Diane and Father Gerard were together.

A teenager reported that she went for confession; when she opened the door to go to the waiting area in the church for Father Gerard, she caught him in a compromising situation with Diane. She reported the situation to Diane's husband, William, but William did not care; he and his wife were in control of the church, and strangely enough, that was enough for him. He did not want to disrupt this solid dominance that he and his betraying wife had in the church.

William, as we have surmised, was in the dark about one thing. As astute as he was, he didn't know that his wife was a witch. Every child the couple had, the child died. They could never save a child, and that left William forlorn and increasingly passive. It never occurred to this decent man that his wife, the children's mother, had murdered all of the five children, offering them as sacrifices.

One day, while he was talking to his dad, Mr. Antoine Boudreaux, William told him, "Dad, you got to help me. I can't handle the funerals anymore. I would like to know where this curse comes from. Is it from my family or my wife's family?"

Mr. Antoine responded, "I didn't want to tell you, but now since you asked, I can take you to Thibodaux in Lunette. He is a man of power. Thibodaux will tell you. He is one of our most powerful vodou priests in the area. Tonight, go to bed early. I will come to wake you up around two o'clock in the morning. On horses, it will take us about three hours to get there."

When the two o'clock cock sang its song, William was already awake and saddled on his horse. His father arrived on his own on horseback. It was so early that even the morning star was still in deep sleep. The moon was still in her black nightgown, sleeping in her chamber. They took off for Lunette.

When they arrived at Thibodaux's, they could not find the entrance of his house. They stood at the fifty-one-acre fence, gazing. All of a sudden, two zombies arrived and asked them, "Are you looking for Papa Thibodaux?"

"Yes," they both replied.

"Let's go!" one of the zombies said.

The zombies took them to the house of Thibodaux. When they arrived at the door, one of the zombies knocked. Then a woman in a long pink robe came to answer the door. When they looked closely, the woman's arms and feet were of a dog's. She told the men, "Please be seated."

His father sat, but William stood and stared at the woman, astounded. He could not believe what he was seeing. Mr. Boudreaux said to William, "Do not be afraid. Everything will be all right."

Then they saw a middle-aged very dark-skinned man appear from out of nowhere and walk directly toward William. "You are here for a family issue?"

"Yes, Papa," William replied.

"Ah, I see your wife killed every child she bore with you."

"My wife killed them?" William asked.

"Yes," Thibodaux replied. "Your wife is an international witch queen. She travels two to three times a week to Cuba, Puerto Rico, and Jamaica for witches' ceremonies. She is very powerful. Did you know that your wife is a witch?"

"No, Papa Thibodaux."

"This is a big case," said Thibodaux. "Your wife is a powerful witch. She can eat you alive if we make any mistakes and if she knows you came here. But I can help you. You need to put thirty-five dollars and thirteen cents down. Then I will reveal to you many things about your wife."

He pulled thirty-five dollars and counted thirteen cents and dropped it on the floor at Thibodaux's feet. William did this because he had learned from his father to never hand money to a vodou priest.

They will not take it. One must put it on the floor. Thibodaux stooped and picked up the money. Then he walked barefoot in his long black robe. His beard almost touched the ground.

He came back with a cup filled with water. He poured some of the water to the left. "Papa Legba, kote w ye (Father Legba, where are you)?" Then some water on the left. "Where are you, mothering Erzulie?" Then he said to William, "You lost five children with your wife, is that true?"

"Wi, Papa (Yes, Father)!" William answered.

"Ah, it will be hard for you to accept, but I can't lie to you. Your wife is the queen of a *bizango* band. Do you believe me?"

"Well, what can I do? I have to accept it."

"Your wife has killed all the children. She is a very powerful witch."

William put his head down. He raised his head. "Oh, Papa Thibodaux, I am shocked. I can't accept that. I wonder if she confesses that to Father Gerard."

Thibodaux intervened. He came closer to William; he raised his head and said, "Do you know that Father Gerard is with your wife?"

"That I know," replied William.

Mr. Antoine looked at William with angry eyes. "William, you know Father Gerard fucked your wife?"

"I am afraid to say it, but yes, Dad!"

"Jesus Christ!" Mr. Antoine pulled the chair back farther against the wall. Then he got up. "What have you done about that, William? Oh, Christ! I don't want to hear this one." Mr. Antoine tried to leave Thibodaux's office.

"You can't leave, Mr. Antoine. There are more things that you need to know," said Thibodaux. Both Thibodaux and Mr. Antoine glanced at one another; they looked at William with compassion.

William was greatly distressed and troubled. Then he raised his head. "Papa Thibodaux, do you think that you can prove to me that my wife is a witch?"

"Do you really want to challenge me, son?"

Then William began to lament. He wept till he was no longer able to weep anymore, then he fell on his stomach, unconscious. After many maneuvers, William awoke. He opened his eyes. He saw Thibodaux standing on his right and his father on his left. He said, "No, I do not believe this one!"

"What is it that you do not believe?" Thibodaux asked.

"Right now I left my wife at home. She is suffering. She never eats." William raised his voice and wept again. His eyes looked tired. He appeared weak after all the dead he has buried.

His dad held him and said, "William, you must be strong. You do not have to grieve so much."

William responded, "Dad, I must weep. My wife is innocent. I know for sure that she is not a witch. I wouldn't marry her if she was. She would never have killed our children."

"Son, I do not want you to plead for your wife. Witches are tricky. They can live with you for a lifetime, and you never discover they are witches, and witchcraft is a vice. Those who practice witchcraft have no pity for no one, including their children, spouse, or friends, and they can't help it."

The son said, "I can't believe you said that, Dad. You mean my wife is a witch? Please take me home. I do not want to hear this, and I will never accept it."

Mr. Boudreaux looked at William. He laughed, then he said, "Son, you will accept it in due time. If you were my age, you would think twice before you say you will never accept it. Even the Bible says, 'Woe to the man who puts his confidence in a man.' Ah, son, let me tell you. You are academically much more prepared than I was, but to know what I know, you have a long way to go."

"Father, I know my wife is not a witch."

"Son, do you know who is a witch? If I tell you your mother is a witch, what would you tell me?"

"Dad, you know what I will tell you. My mother is not a witch."

"I see, but I am going to tell you this once and for all, never trust a man, even me and your mother. Trust God. I don't go to church, but I know God is the only one on this earth to trust."

Thibodaux sat there on his wide chair with his two bodyguards, who were two powerful zombies, one on his right and the other on his left. He listened to everything William and his father said. He did not say a word.

When William and his father completed their talk, he said to William, "I wish you listen to your father. Do you want to know who I am, sir? Do you think I can lie to you?"

"Oh, Papa Thibodaux! I would never say that you lied to me."

Thibodaux turned into a snake and went under William's legs.

William jumped. "Oh god!"

Thibodaux turned back to normal, and he laughed. "Would you believe me now?"

"Wi, Papa (Yes, Father)," William answered in Creole.

Thibodaux changed his face into the face of a horse. Then he changed to himself again and said to William, "I know that you are grieving, but I do not like to deal with weak men. You got to be stronger. I have dealt with your father in the past. He is a strong man." Mr. Boudreaux shook his head. Thibodaux continued, "For me to help you catch your wife, you must be strong."

"Yes, Father Thibodaux. I promise you I will be strong."

Thibodaux said to both men, "Close your eyes." They closed their eyes. "Open your eyes," Thibodaux asked them.

They opened their eyes, and they sat in a new place where a bunch of women was dancing, and men were laughing, drinking, and smoking. The place was so beautiful; both men were confused as to where they were.

Thibodaux said to the men, "Close your eyes."

They closed their eyes and found themselves with Thibodaux again when they opened their eyes.

Then William asked Mr. Boudreaux, "Where were we?"

"I do not think we were in Haiti," responded Mr. Boudreaux.

Thibodaux said to William, "I was going to help you discover who your wife really is, but you are too weak of a man for me to do so."

"No, Majesty," he addressed Thibodaux with utter sincerity. "After all the marvelous powers you have demonstrated, now I can handle anything."

Thibodaux was pleased but still skeptical about the strength of William. Thibodaux spoke directly to William. "If you have to do this, you have to be wise. If you get angry or get emotional, she can easily catch you. I will give you something to drink so that you won't be too emotional because you are going to deal with a cunning and powerful woman. If you're not strong or emotionally prepared, you might be her next victim."

He handed a jar full of hot pepper to William. "Take this!"

William took it. "What do I do with this, Papa Thibodaux?"

"Wait for a minute! Why are you so in a hurry? Where are you going?" Thibodaux questioned William with humor.

Mr. Boudreaux laughed. "Now he believes in you, Papa Thibodaux."

Thibodaux smiled. "He better believe in me." Thibodaux looked at both men and said, "I am going to tell you what to do, but if you fail, even the Protestants can't save you from your wife. She will eat you with her *bizango* band.

"If you are wise, you will discover your wife. Just follow the instructions that I will give you. Your wife is a cruel woman. I know you won't believe me because she is very smart. She knows how to manipulate you, but you will find out soon. She appears to be a woman of wisdom. She is nice and has a nice smile. She appears very kind. I am looking at her right now. Do you want to see her?" Thibodaux asked the men.

Both men responded, "Yes, please."

Thibodaux pulled a mirror. Then he performed his prayer, and then Diane appeared in the mirror, talking to one of the neighbors. "I could kill her right now if I wanted to. This woman that she is talking to right now, she is a witch too," said Thibodaux.

Thibodaux continued, "The hot pepper I gave you is to put on her skin. You must kill her before she kills you. Look at you! You are a very young man, but what she put you through makes you get old fast."

Thibodaux handed a little black bottle to William. "Before you go to bed, drink from this and then wash yourself with the rest." Thibodaux also handed a piece of paper to William. "Recite this before you go to bed. You will see things that you never had dreamt of seeing."

William took everything from Thibodaux. "I thank you very much, Papa Thibodaux. I promise to do everything you have asked me to do."

"You better do what I asked you to do. Listen! Your wife is powerful. If she realizes you came over here to speak to me, she will kill you because she would be afraid. In fact, you need to show her with more love than ever before. Give her the best of you in bed. Try to memorize the prayer that I gave you. Pray it in your heart when you are in bed with her. She will try to put you to sleep, but you won't sleep. However, pretend that you are sleeping when she starts her ceremony. You need to put the jar of hot pepper in a place that she won't see it. The first thing that she will do when she is leaving to go to her *bizango*, she will pull her skin off and open it like it was her wet nightgown. Then she will fly away. When she does that, take the hot pepper and spread it all over the skin."

On that day, when William got home, his father said, "William, be careful. Remember what Thibodaux told you. I will see you tomorrow. Call me if you encounter any problems."

"Everything will be fine, Dad."

Early that afternoon, William looked for some strong leaves. He boiled tea. He drank them, and then he went to bed with his wife. Once he began to caress his wife and prepared himself to penetrate, Diane said, "I feel like we have intercourse for no reason."

"Why do you say that, darling?" William responded. "If we can't save any children, what is the use of having sex?" Then she began to cry. "Do not cry, darling," said William. "God will answer our prayer. I believe that his judgment is closer than we think."

"What do you mean by his judgment, darling?"

"What I mean is that we have persecution, but I trust God to win the battle."

"I believe so too, darling," replied Diane.

Then they turned off the light. About ten minutes after the lights were turned off; Diane pretended that she was asleep. William did the same. She put her ear close to William's nose to listen. Then she made her witch's prayer while she crossed William three times to put him into a deep sleep. When she thought that William was sound asleep, she was able to turn into a skeleton. She pulled two chairs out and then put them together. She was easily able to take off her skin and put it open wide on the two chairs like a nightgown.

She turned into a peregrine falcon. She grew a tail, her feet turned into bird's legs. She grew wings and feathers. She beat her wings together, and then the roof opened automatically for her. She flew through the roof, and then the roof closed back.

William shook when he saw that. He got up and ran out. He saw his wife continue to take off like an airplane. She traveled about two hundred miles per hour.

He went back to the house. He took the jar of hot pepper that Thibodaux gave him; he took a big spoon, spread the hot pepper throughout the skin, and left the skin exactly as it was on the chair.

That night, his wife flew to Puerto Rico to attend a programming meeting for a big ceremony that they were going to have in December. Diane no longer has children to share. This December, William was going to be her victim.

She arrived at the ceremony in Puerto Rico. They ate and danced. Then they sat down. Each one of the witches promised something for this big ceremony. It shall be big because most of the witches in the West Indies will attend this year. Diane promised to sacrifice her husband. After William finished spreading the hot pepper on the skin, he went back to bed.

Diane finished her ceremony; she flew back to Haiti. Around four o'clock in the morning, William saw the roof open wide. She descended. As soon as Diane entered, she took her skin and put it back on her as if she was putting her nightgown on. Then she began to say to herself. "Diane, this is not your skin. Oh, Diane, this is not my skin." She crossed William three times, thinking that he was sleep, to awake him. "Oh, Diane! This is not my skin!" She called, "William, William, this is not my skin!"

William pretended he did not know what was going on. He asked, "Diane, what is going on?"

"This is not my skin!"

"What?"

"Diane, this is not my skin!"

"What are you talking about?" William asked.

"Ah, I am hot, William. This cannot be my skin!"

"What skin are you talking about?" William turned on the light.

Diane ran out. William knocked at the neighbors' door and told them that Diane was going crazy. He did not know what was going on with her. Diane ran to the river and jumped into the cold water. Then she ran back out.

"Oh, Diane, this is not my skin!"

All her witch partners who were with her just less than an hour ago, flying from Puerto Rico, wondered among themselves, *What is going on with, Diane? Did she eat some poisoned food?*

One of the witches approached closer to Diane's ear while four men held her. "Diane, what happened?"

Diane responded, "I don't know, but this is not my skin."

Father Gerard arrived at the scene. "Diane, oh, Diane, what is happening?"

"Oh God," responded Diane. "I am sorry, Father Gerard. I am sorry." She opened her arms; she was naked. "Oh, Father Gerard, this is not my skin."

Tears were coming down from Father Gerard's eyes. "Oh, sister, you look terrible. What's happening? Confess to me."

Diane looked at Father Gerard for a moment. She is suffering. She is out of breath. "Father Gerard, I am a witch, and this is not Diane's skin."

"Oh, Sister Diane, you are not a witch. Confess to me, please. What is happening?"

There was a minute of silence. The sisters from Notre Dame of Lower Gandou arrived all in black. They came closer to Diane. "What is going on, Diane?"

"Oh, sisters," Diane responded, "this is not Diane's skin."

Mr. William was standing at a distance from Diane; he stayed calm though he looked like someone who had not slept for weeks. Father Gerard took a glance at William, and then he moved toward him.

"William, what's happening? Confess to me. You have been silent throughout this ordeal."

William responded, "Father Gerard, I am shocked. It is the devil who killed my wife."

"Who killed her?" Father Gerard responded.

"My wife was a witch. Father, she was a professional witch." William covered his face and stooped down on the sand by the river. He raised his head and looked at Father Gerard straight in the eyes. "Did she ever tell you that she was a witch during confession?"

"I can't tell you what she confesses to me. I am sorry." Father Gerard moved away.

The sister moved toward William. "Oh, William, what did you do to Diane? Oh, William, confess to us."

William responded, "I will talk to Father Gerard during confession." Then he moved away from the sisters.

After four hours of lamenting and weeping, Diane fell and died.

Mr. Boudreaux arrived. "What happened? William, did we get her?"

Right away, everyone suspected that William had done something to his wife. The news went fast that she was the witch that killed all her children. Thibodaux gave William the secret to catching his wife. Then the other witches began to persecute William and Mr. Boudreaux.

One of the witches slapped William. "Did you poison Diane? Tell me, vagabond!"

During the funeral, all the witches were dressed in white. They wanted to show people in the area that they are strong, and no one can stop them.

The day after the funeral, they went to William's house and spent the night in the yard chanting, lamenting, and dancing. In the morning, one of the women came to William and said, "We are going to dance at your house until we cook you in December."

One night, they went to Antoine Boudreaux's house and began to throw stones. They killed one of Boudreaux's cows, and then they called, "Boudreaux, if you think Thibodaux can save you, come out! Come out, Boudreaux!"

Boudreaux, his children, and his wife got scared. Once Boudreaux got up, he went straight to William's home. "William, we are not going to win over those vampires. We got to go back to Thibodaux."

"Father, I was going to call you to ask for the same thing. I did not sleep at night. I am sick. We need to go now."

"Okay. Let's go!"

They saddled their horses and went back to see Thibodaux. They arrived; they stood at the house as they did before. Then two zombies came to get them. One of them went and knocked at Thibodaux's door. A woman came in a long red dress to open the door.

"Be seated, please," the woman said.

They sat. Then Thibodaux arrived. "Men, I know why you are here this time. You have been persecuted by the witches, but I can't do anything for you. They are too many, and they are very powerful. In fact, they already have your soul in their hands." He pointed to William. "The only person who can help you in this situation now is God only. You can go to church, call a pastor to come to pray with you."

They left as soon as they got home. They went straight to Mr. Boudreaux's house and called Pastor Gabriel to pray for them. Pastor Gabriel prayed for William and Mr. Boudreaux's family.

After Pastor Gabriel prayed for them, he read John 1:12 that says, "But as many as received by him, he gave them power to be made the sons of God, to them that believe in his name."

Pastor Gabriel told them that they are now children of God. Vodou, witchcraft, and all other powers cannot bother them more, for now, they are in Christ Jesus. He also told them that the Bible says, "Anyone, for the old life is gone, a new life has begun! They are not the same anymore for the one life is gone, a new life has begun! Therefore, they do not have to fear anymore. It is important that they understand that as long as they stay in the bosom of Christ, all evil forces will run away."

Then Pastor Gabriel told them to read Psalm 46 every night before they go to bed. He also encouraged William to stay with his dad since he does not have a wife then. So every night, William and his dad, his mother, and the other children prayed together. Then they read Psalm 46:

God is our refuge and strength,
an ever-present help in trouble.
² Therefore we will not fear, though the earth give way
and the mountains fall into the heart of the sea,
³ though its waters roar and foam
and the mountains quake with their surging.[c]
⁴ There is a river whose streams make glad the city of God,
the holy place where the Most High dwells.
⁵ God is within her, she will not fall;
God will help her at break of day.
⁶ Nations are in uproar, kingdoms fall;
he lifts his voice, the earth melts.
⁷ The LORD Almighty is with us;
the God of Jacob is our fortress.
⁸ Come and see what the LORD has done,
the desolations he has brought on the earth.
⁹ He makes wars cease
to the ends of the earth.
He breaks the bow and shatters the spear;
he burns the shields[d] with fire.
¹⁰ He says, "Be still, and know that I am God;
I will be exalted among the nations,
I will be exalted in the earth."
¹¹ The LORD Almighty is with us;
the God of Jacob is our fortress.

Three days after they were converted, two of the witches came to Mr. Boudreaux's house, saying, "Please pray for us. We are going to die. We want your God. We came here last night. We saw a big army surrounding your house. A man told us we all need to repent, or we are going to die."

The two witches that were persecuting and demonizing the other witches that wanted to change their lives, Siamese and Sylvia, fate took their lives. Death came to them that day. Once that was known by the two and the other witches, three more women came to proclaim the

Christian God. One of Mr. Boudreaux's younger sons went to get Pastor Gabriel. This was a highly unusual situation. Followers of vodou were surrendering to the grace and salvation of Jesus Christ.

The pastor arrived at Mr. Boudreau's house, and along with them and two other men who joined them, they prayed with intensity and gratefulness for and with the five witches. They accepted Christ and testified of how much evil that they had done in the commune of Bainet.

The last time I went to Bainet, I saw both Mr. Boudreaux and William singing a duet. The song says, "I am not serving Satan no more. Praise the Lord! I am not going to consult vodou priests anymore. Praise the Lord! I am not going to offer sacrifice to false gods no more, praise the Lord! Glory to God who saves me. Praise the Lord!"

Come to His Light

I still hear the vodou drums of my ancestors in my ears,

But I fear no more of Ogoun demanding me black animals.

I will not set the flame for Marinèt to dance on fire,

And I still hear my aunts shaking the *asson* for Ghede to enter. But I fear no more who will die in the next sacrifice.

I am now living in Christ Jesus, the king of Israel.

I do not fear Haitians' craftiness to do evil to one another. But now I can see the Haitians' inability to see their pitfalls. I think of that vodou priest burning money, the poor die hungry. Tell me now, why do I cry for my ancestors' misery? If they would take my advice, they would have stood tall like me. They would reject their vodou gods and acquire God's grace. I fear no more of black magic, the wealth my ancestors brought from Africa.

JOSEPH P. POLICAPE

Come, take my god and live like me, free and happy forever after. Vodou and magic bring nothing but fear, poverty, and deceptions. Vodou and magic bring nothing more to mankind but insecurity. Stop living in confusion! Stop living as the miserable of this planet. In Christ Jesus, there is no shadow of darkness. Come to his light!

There are many families or *nanchons* (nations) of loa: Rada, Petro, Nago, Kongo, and Ghede, and many others.

Rada loa

The Rada loa are older spirit from Arica and the kingdom of Dahomey. The Rada loa are mainly water spirits and many of the Rada loa are served with water. The Rada are cool or calm because they are less aggressive than the Petro. They include Legba, Loko, Ayizan, Damballa Wedo, and Ayida-Weddo, and Erzulie Fréda Dahomey, La Sirène, and Agwé. Many of these spirits are served with white, sometimes in conjunction with another color. For example, Danbala may take white and green in some vodou houses, or just white in others. Freda may take white and pink in one house, or pink and light blue in another. However, as a rule of thumb, white is a color appropriate to all the Rada.

Petro loa

The Petro loa are generally the more fiery, occasionally aggressive and warlike loa, and are associated with Haiti and the New World. They include Ezili Dantor, Marinette, and Met Kalfu (Maitre Carrefour, "Master Crossroads"). Their traditional color is red. As with the Rada, additional colors may be associated with individual Petro. Dantor will be served with red, but in different houses may additionally take navy blue, green, or gold.

Kongo loa

Originating from the Congo region, these loa include the many Simbi loa. It also includes Marinette, a fierce and much-feared female loa.

Nago loa

Originating from Yorubaland, this nation includes many of the Ogoun loa, most of whom use "Ogou" as a sort of family name. Examples include Ogou Feray, a martial soldier loa; Ogou Bdagris, a wiser general; Ogou Panama, often viewed as a pilot (and an example of how loa can subdivide as the world changes); and Ogou Balendjo, who serves on the ship of the Rada ocean loa Agwe.

For the purpose of this book, we will only list the loa mention in these tales.

Papa Legba

An old man carrying a crutch and a round straw bag. He smokes a pipe and always enjoys smoking his pipe. According to the legend, he is the loa that open the crossroad to allow communication with the spirits. He is from the Rada nation, and he associates with saints Lazarus and Anthony of Padua. His favorite colors are red, white, brown, purple, and gold. He likes to be served on Monday or Thursday in March. His choices of foods are popcorn, rice, black coffee, and he enjoys his rum.

Danbala-Wedo

Of the Rada nation and he associates with saints Moses with the Ten Commandments and Saint Patrick of Ireland. He serves on Thursday in April. He is a python snake. His favorite color is pure white. His meal has to be white, such as white rice, white bread, etc., on white plates. His concepts are purity, coolness, and peace.

Ayida-Wedo

Belong to the Rada nation. Saint Miraculous (Our Lady of the Miraculous Medal). She serves on Thursday in any month of the year. Her favorite colors are white or pastel rainbow colors. Her meal has to be white, such as white rice, white bread, and *akasan*. Her symbols are the rainbow, snake, and sky. Like Danbala, her concept is coolness, purity, rainbow, and peace.

Met AgweTawoyo

The nation is Rada, associates with Saint Ulrich, Archangel Raphael (both holding fish). He serves on Thursday in the month of May. He enjoys food such as champagne, coffee with cream and sugar, rice boiled in sweet milk, melon, cakes with blue-and-white icing, whole fish, white rooster, and white rams or goats. His symbol is a boat or a ship, and his concept is the ocean with everything in it.

La Sirène

The nation is Rada, and she associates with Saint Diosa del Mar (Mother of the Sea) or Our Lady of Charity (Caridad del Cobre in Spanish). She can be served on any Thursday in May or other months. Gifts that must be given to her are perfume, champagne, mirror, seashells or pearls, silver cones or jewelry, rice boiled in sweet milk, whole fish, and cakes with blue-and-white icing. Her symbols are the mermaid, whale, and dolphin; and her concepts are abundance, fertility, beauty, murmuring, wealth, and water.

Erzulie Freda

She is from the Rada nation, but can also be considered to be a part of the New World. She associates with Saint Miraculous (Our Lady of Sorrow). She likes to be served on Thursday in the month of June. She likes gifts such as perfume, mirrors, cosmetics, fine jewelry, luxury items, fine candies, fancy cookies, cakes with white or pink frosting, baked fish, and champagne. Her symbols are heart, gold, and jewelry; and her concepts are love and desire

Brave Ghede
Nation Rada

He is the guardian and watchman of the graveyard. He keeps the dead souls in and the living souls out. He is sometimes considered an aspect of Nibo.

Azaka
Nation: Rada

Loa de Tonnerre (also Azaca or Azacca) is a loa of thunder in Vodou, He is in the same "family" as Azaka Medeh, the loa of harvest. His day of the week is Thursday. He likes the color blue and brown and his foods are spicy foods, rums, and his cigar.

Ogou Feray
Nation: Rada

Haitians believe Ogun is a warrior, a hunter who fights for the innocent. His symbols are dog and iron, and he is associated with Saint James. His food is as simple as spicy meats, and strong black coffee.

Simbi Dlo
Nation: Petro

Sim'bi is a large and diverse family of serpents, also known as loa in Haitian vodou. He likes to be served on Tuesdays. He associates with Saint John the Baptist. His colors are white and green. His symbols are snakes and water. His offerings are a pipe of tobacco, and spicy pork, goat, or chicken.

Erzile Danto

Petro Loa

Ezilí Dantor or Erzulie Dantó is the main of the Petro family in Haitian vodou.

Tuesdays are the days to be served. She is considered to be a tough loa because she rarely cries. Like her sister Freda, she is more uncomplicated in terms of the offerings she requires. She likes strong black coffee with her bread and spicy food. Her colors are white, black, blue, or purple.

Baron Samedi

He is from the Ghede nation. He is associated with Saints: Gabriel Expedite. He eats very spicy food, smokes a cigarette, and wears a top hat and sunglasses. His symbols are crosses and cemeteries.

REFERENCE

Rigaud, Milo. 1985. *Secrets of Voodoo.* City Lights Book.

No, F., & Rare, C. (1948). From Wikipedia, the free encyclopedia. *age.*

INDEX

9 781664 175167